TEQUILA FOUR

An Althea Rose Novel

TRICIA O'MALLEY

Lovewrite Publishing

Cover Design:
Alchemy Book Covers
Editor:
Elayne Morgan

"There's a man going around taking names. And he decides who to free and who to blame. Everybody won't be treated all the same."

– Johnny Cash

Chapter One

"I'M NEVER TOUCHING another man so long as I live," I vowed, plucking another grape from a gold and silver bowl set on Luna's white-washed counter. Luna snorted, shaking her blonde hair as she breezed past me to hand a beautifully wrapped package of magickly brewed lavender soaps to a woman who stood just inside the front door waiting. A regular customer from the fancy-schmancy side of Tequila Key – which the rich liked to call Port Atticus – Mrs. Brewster slipped into our store once a month for Luna's healing elixirs and soaps. She had a standing order, which allowed her to spend only a minimal amount of time in the shop – so as not to be seen, naturally, and have her reputation tarnished.

I had no idea why. It wasn't like coming to the Luna Rose Potions & Tarot Shop was slumming, exactly. At least not on Luna's side of the shop. I'd gone into business with Luna years ago, as our otherworldly talents complemented each other delightfully. It didn't hurt that we were best friends as well.

But no one would call us two peas in a pod. I leaned against the counter and surveyed Luna's side of the store – all white on white on white. If elegance were a fragrance, it would be the scent of the shop. Beautifully wrapped soaps, healing tonics in white and gold bottles, and tables full of stunning crystals were artfully arranged against a backdrop of white. A few of my underwater photographs – a hobby of mine, which helped me decompress – were delicately framed, offering small splashes of color around the room.

Even the screen dividing our shops was delicate. Its gold wire etching and pretty cherry blossom design effectively separated our respective spaces. And thank goodness for that, because stepping from Luna's side of the shop to mine was like going from the symphony to a Guns N' Roses concert. I'd learned long ago that it was best to meet people's expectations of a psychic tarot card reader. My side of the shop was an explosion of velvets and leopard prints, with hundreds of mystical trinkets and antiquities tucked on the shelves lining the wall. Herman, my skeleton, sported a Ramones shirt, and lounged on a leopard-print chair in the corner. Though I drew the line at wearing a turban and caftan, my shop reinforced almost all the expectations of a tarot card reader.

I'd briefly tried changing it up years ago – all soothing tones and elegant leather furniture, much like a lawyer's office. My business had all but dried up. It seems people want to experience the unfamiliar, and if Herman staring at them slack-jawed from the corner and a crystal ball on the table keeps them coming back, then I'm more than happy to oblige.

I never was much for soothing tones anyway, I thought as I ran my hand through my riot of dark curls. I'd recently changed out the caramel streaks for a screamingly hot pink, and had added an under-layer of deep purple.

I'm not saying the change in hair color was to rebel against my on-again-off-again boyfriend's proper upbringing. But since we were kind of off again, I'd decided to go dramatic with the hair.

"Does that ever bother you?" I asked Luna as she waved goodbye to Mrs. Brewster from the front door. Turning, she cocked her head at me in question. "You know, the women who can barely deign to step foot in your shop?"

"Ah well, that's their problem – not mine. I'd hate to be encumbered by society like that, being so worried about what people think – well, just think of all the fun we'd miss out on," Luna said, rounding the counter and tucking the receipt into a pretty file folder decorated with gold filigree. I studied the slim column of white silk that fell in a line from her chest, with only a dainty gold moon pendant breaking up the flow. Everything about Luna was dainty – from the smooth sweep of her cheek to her slim build, she was the antithesis of my curves, boisterous hair, and loud personality.

But don't let her delicateness fool you. Housed inside that tiny body is a power that I certainly wouldn't trifle with. Being a white witch meant that Luna never caused harm to others, but that didn't mean she couldn't redirect the course of fate once in a while.

"I suppose you're right. It must be exhausting to live with such constant restrictions," I agreed, annoyance lacing my voice as I popped another grape in my mouth. Societal restrictions were currently the cause of grief between me and Cash, my insanely hot and indescribably wealthy boyfriend, well, *kind-of* boyfriend.

"Is that why you're swearing off men? Too many rules come with dating Cash?" Luna asked, arching a perfectly shaped brow in my direction.

"That, and I don't know where things sit with Trace after the Valentine's Day party a few weeks ago, and Cash got weird about it and then had to leave for a big job and, well, I haven't really heard from either of them. So, screw men," I said, shoving another grape in my mouth to stem the flow of words. And to stop me from venting all my anger in one fell swoop.

When it comes to being angry I much prefer the slow burn instead of a flash in the pan. Not that I would advise being near me when that slow burn catches fire.

"You could screw both of them, you know," Luna suggested lightly, making me laugh – which I'm sure was her intent.

"And what would that make me? Just the kind of woman Cash's family thinks I am."

"You don't know for sure what they think. And speaking of screwing – screw that stupid sister of his. She was entirely too rude and judgmental. Miss New York can stay right where she is. We're doing just fine down here in sleepy Tequila Key." Luna infused her words with a dash of southern backwater drawl.

"That's right, us swamp folks sure do know how to have ourselves a good time," I drawled back at her, and we both laughed, the mood considerably lightened.

Not that Tequila Key actually has a swamp, but it's certainly one of the sleepier Keys on the way down to the party town of Key West. Merely a speed-bump along the way, with a sign proclaiming "Tequila Makes It Better" along the highway, we're an often-overlooked stop in the Keys. Which suits me just fine – I'd grown up here and I loved my little town, though we'd seen many changes in recent years as Tequila Key was discovered by developers and the town's founding family, the Whittiers, had worked out a tax break for rich folk to come down and buy themselves some land. Soon our town had been divided into the new and old parts, with the main street being a neutral zone.

Okay, I'm being dramatic. It's not like it's a war zone between the newly relocated rich people of Port Atticus – the "new" side of Tequila Key – and the old town. But, well, I'm cranky today.

So sue me.

"Is Cash still mad about you making out with Trace?" Luna asked, coming back from our detour to focus on the original subject matter.

"He claims to understand that I had ingested a love potion, but every time he says the words 'love potion' he gets a little tic below his eye," I said.

"What else do you pick up on?" Luna asked, referencing my psychic abilities.

So here's the deal – for the most part, I try not to dip into people's thoughts or read people's futures unintentionally. First off, because it's rude, and secondly, if I listened in on every internal conversation that people were having, it would feel like the entire town was shouting at me.

Putting walls up and keeping them firmly in place keeps me on the right side of sanity.

"I haven't listened in. Too much, I should say; I haven't listened in too much." I shrugged and grabbed another grape. "But I'm getting a lot of confusion from him. Confusion about his feelings, anger at me, and anger at himself for not being able to ignore his family as much as he'd like to."

"Ah, I suppose that's frustrating. The expectations of family are often our biggest constraints," Luna nodded, studiously eyeing the bowl before picking one perfectly plump grape from the bunch.

"I guess I wouldn't know," I said.

"Most people didn't grow up like you did, Althea," Luna laughed at me. "With a world-famous psychic for a mother and a music professor for a father, I'd say you've been raised as non-traditionally as possible. The only constraint I see imposed upon you is to never become normal or mainstream."

We both shuddered at the thought.

"Mom sends her love, by the way. She says she knows you're trying to pin her down, but she'll talk to you when she's ready," I said. Luna had been trying to get a hold of my mother once she'd discovered that I carried more magick than either of us had originally known.

"Abigail's a wily one," Luna grumbled.

"She is at that. I suspect we'll know more when we're meant to know more," I said, turning as the golden fall of delicate bells hanging from the front door tinkled a visitor's arrival.

I raised an eyebrow at the woman who stepped inside,

her eyes scanning past the goods on the table and landing on us. She wasn't here to shop, I decided, as I took in her appearance.

With blonde hair slicked back in a tight chignon, black-framed glasses that suited her sharply angled face, and lips coated in a shiny red gloss, she was all woman. A demure blue silk tank was tucked into a tightly fitted leather pencil skirt and I was momentarily sidetracked by the thought of wearing leather in this heat. Didn't she sweat? Who wore leather skirts in the humidity of the Keys? Cotton, linen, and silks were our friends here.

The woman stopped in front of me and trailed her eyes over what I considered my uniform – a flowy maxi dress in a pretty pattern of black and silver – and tilted her head to the side in question.

"Althea Rose?" she asked, her voice warm but firm.

"The one and only," I said, smiling brightly at her to see if she would smile back.

She didn't.

"My boss has requested that you provide readings for him and his friends on his yacht tomorrow afternoon." The woman didn't phrase it as a question and I took it as it was meant – an order.

"Your name is…?" I said, leaning back and snagging another grape to pop in my mouth nonchalantly as I allowed myself to get a read on this woman.

"Victoria Lavish," she said smoothly. She didn't offer her hand and I didn't hold mine out either. Victoria ignored Luna entirely, keeping her ice blue eyes trained on me.

"Well, Victoria, I have clients tomorrow afternoon. I'm afraid you can't waltz in at a moment's notice and expect me to be free to give your boss and his buddies some readings. Despite what you may think, I run a highly ethical and very professional business." I smiled a bit to take the edge off the words.

"My boss doesn't take no for an answer," Victoria said, a faint line of annoyance showing up on her forehead before it was quickly smoothed over. This time I had no trouble dipping in her head to find out just who her boss was.

"Chadwick Harrington?" I murmured, deliberately allowing Victoria to understand that I'd read her mind, subtly shifting the power back to me. "No clue, though the name sounds familiar."

Victoria rolled her eyes very dramatically and I shot Luna a look over my shoulder.

"He's the head of a big pharma company. I believe he's been in the headlines as of late," Luna said demurely, smoothing out a stack of papers on the counter.

"Yes, well, just a little nonsense is all. Chadwick Charles Harrington is from one of the oldest families in New York. He doesn't need to be exposed to all that press drama. He's come down here to spend some time on the yacht and escape it all. He feels that psychic tarot readings," Victoria crinkled her nose at that, "would be a fun afternoon diversion."

"Is that so? Well, while I certainly am dying to be the entertainment, I'll have to go ahead and say a big no to that one," I said, dismissing this woman and her boss quickly.

"He's offering ten thousand dollars in compensation," Victoria said, and I paused.

"That's a lot of money for a reading. Just how many people will Althea be reading?" Luna asked.

"Only a few," Victoria said dismissively.

Something was not right about this situation. Unfortunately, I have this delightful little trait: When I smell a rat, I have to figure out what's behind it. Which meant that, sure enough, I'd be on that boat tomorrow. Excuse me – yacht.

"Cash up front," I drawled, leaning back and crossing my arms over my chest.

"Half up front and half after the readings," Victoria countered, already reaching into the satchel at her side.

"All up front," I said with a sweet smile on my face. Victoria paused and met my eyes. I held her gaze until she dropped it, muttering under her breath, and pulled a wad of cash from her purse.

"Fine, but don't tell Chadwick I did that," Victoria said, slapping the cash into my palm and turning to leave. It was the first time I'd read fear from her, and that was something I was going to have to seriously consider.

Who was this Chadwick Harrington and why was an ass-kicker like Victoria afraid of him?

Chapter Two

"DOLLA DOLLA BILLS, Y'ALL," Luna hooted out after Victoria had breezed from the room, her expensive perfume lingering for a moment behind her.

"Time to go shoe shopping," I decided, looking down at the stack of money in my hand.

"Or we can finally take that spa trip we've been wanting to do," Luna pointed out.

"For what? You already do all the magickal rituals you need to look fantastic," I scoffed at Luna as I fluttered the bills in my hands.

"For stress relief," Luna sniffed delicately, and I laughed.

"Because you are so stressed?"

"A lady never needs an excuse to go the spa," Luna demurred and I gave up, my mind already circling back to the questions I had.

"First of all, can we just talk about the leather skirt?" I decided to get the easiest out of the way and Luna squealed in response.

"I know! In this heat? What is she thinking?"

"She's wound tight and I have to imagine the leather is not helping," I said.

"Girl needs to loosen the bun and throw on a linen dress. Maybe she wouldn't be so uptight," Luna said.

"I think it would take more than letting her hair down for that one to unwind. If anyone needs a trip to the spa to de-stress, it's her."

"I wonder what she does for Chadwick," Luna said, and I realized that although Victoria had given us her name, she hadn't told us her role on the yacht. Which led me to my second question.

"Do all people who own a yacht always refer to it as a yacht? Do you think they ever just say, 'hey, come hang on the boat'?" I asked.

We both considered it for a moment.

"Nope," we said in unison and laughed.

"It's always 'yacht,' no matter what," Luna said.

"Ladies… could I interest you, in, you know, coming back to my yacht?" I deepened my voice and pretended to be a country club dude.

"Ladies… want to rock my boat?" Luna chimed in, and I hooted with laughter.

"Ladies… can I be the captain of your ship?" I responded and we both doubled over in laughter. Straightening, I wiped my eyes and caught my breath.

"In all seriousness, though, I'm not sure if you should go on this yacht," Luna said, her pretty features scrunched in concern.

"Tell me about this Chadwick Charles Harrington. Sounds like someone I would hate," I said.

"He is, literally, the worst," Luna said and glanced at a slim gold watch on her wrist. Where I just looked at my iPhone for the time, Luna still wore watches.

"Let's go get a margarita. You're going to need to settle in for this. Plus, I promised Miss Elva I'd give her some of the new labradorite crystal I got in today."

"I'll pick her up after I let Hank out. See you in a half hour," I called, already on my way out the door to where my beach cruiser was locked in front of the shop, my mind still whirling with questions about this Chadwick Harrington and his little servant, Victoria.

Look, I'm not going to try and imply that my life is normal. In fact, it's been particularly eventful over the past six months or so. But typically, on a day-to-day basis, I spend my time reading cards for clients, scuba diving with Trace, taking underwater photographs for my blog, and fulfilling the picture orders that come in through the website. I'm not saying we don't get a slew of colorful characters making their way through Tequila Key, because, well, it's the Keys. But all my spidey-senses were tingling in regards to Victoria and her yacht-boy.

It was another beautiful day in Tequila Key, the sun heading towards the horizon, but still a couple hours of light left before it dipped beneath the ocean. I waved to some neighbors as I biked down my street to my house, a semi-detached at the end of a row of colorful houses. When I'd first seen the place, I wasn't sure if I'd wanted to share a wall with another home. But when the realtor had shown me the privacy fence in the back yard and the secret slice of beachfront property it concealed, I'd put money down on the spot. Here's a tip: If you find waterfront access in the Keys – and I don't mean on a canal – buy it. You'll always make your money back. I'd had sand put in to create a real beach, and my Boston terrier, Hank, loved racing down to the water to bark at any fish he could find.

As I approached my house, two pointy ears peeked over the windowsill by the door and I smiled. Hank had some sort of internal timer that always allowed him to know when I was home. Unlocking the front door, I pushed it open and bent automatically to pet the wriggling sausage that was Hank.

"Ready to go outside, buddy?" I asked, and Hank raced through the downstairs. When I'd moved in, I had knocked out all the walls and created a huge open layout, with the kitchen, dining area, and sitting areas all in one space. Then I'd used my wild, kitschy sense of design to create little conversation corners and nooks through the room. You could find everything from a red leather chair to a suit of armor on my first floor. My underwater photographs dominated the walls here, adding even more color and depth to the room.

I crossed the room and unlocked the sliding glass door so Hank could race outside and take care of business. I glanced down at my dress and decided there was no need to change. We were just going to the tiki bar. Which reminded me – I needed to call Miss Elva.

I stepped onto my back porch and tossed a ball for a delirious Hank as I waited for Miss Elva to pick up.

"Well, isn't this a surprise? I could've sworn you'd gone and moved out of town," Miss Elva said immediately, and I winced.

"I'm sorry I haven't been in touch. A lot going on, I

guess."

"Sho, and Rafe and I were beginning to think you were working yourself up to a good head of mad after the Valentine's Day party." Miss Elva's silky smooth voice had a hint of accusation to it.

"I'm not mad at you. Rafe, I'm going to have some words with. It's just been a tough couple weeks with Cash, and I kind of just focused on taking care of my business, I guess," I said, bending to pick the ball up for Hank again.

"You plan on telling me 'bout it?" Miss Elva demanded.

"I'm picking you up in a few minutes to go to Lucky's. You'll hear all about it. And about someone named Chadwick Harrington that I'm going to be doing readings for tomorrow."

I heard Miss Elva's swift intake of breath.

"You've heard of him?"

"Child, the whole country has heard of him. Don't you watch the news?"

"Apparently I've had my head buried in the sand," I said, tossing the ball for an exuberant Hank again.

"We've got a lot to talk about. I'll see you soon."

"And tell that ghost of yours to steer clear of me, or I'll send him back through the veil," I bit out. I heard Miss Elva chuckle as I hung up.

"Stupid pirate ghost messing up my stupid love life," I muttered to Hank, and he grinned at me, his tongue lolling out of his mouth.

"Let's get you fed," I said and smiled as Hank danced after me, his favorite part of the day almost near.

If only I were that easy to please.

Chapter Three

MISS ELVA KNEW how to make an impression. I should take notes from her. Hell, famous runway models should probably take notes from her. I've never known anyone who carried themselves with the level of confidence and air of unconcern that Miss Elva consistently achieved. I honestly couldn't say if I've ever even seen her ruffled.

The woman was unflappable.

Perhaps her considerable magickal powers – old magick, you get me? – and being a voodoo priestess had a lot to do with it. But, as a woman, she carried herself like she knew her own worth. And turned every head in the room by doing so.

I pulled up to her house – one of the few on this street with a second story – and she was posed at the top of the stairs waiting for me. Miss Elva didn't just laze around. She posed, she perched, she reclined, but she most notably did not slump, waddle, or whimper her way anywhere in life.

Today's caftan was a brilliant orange shot through with streaks of red and white beading, creating a sunset-like effect. A matching scarf was wound around her head and silver earrings dripped in columns straight to her shoulders. Miss Elva wears caftans almost exclusively, and I can't say I blame her, considering my maxi-dress addiction. They're easy, they make you look great, and if you eat too much at dinner you don't need to pop the button on your jeans.

"Looking smashing as always, Miss Elva," I called through the window, and she threw her head back and laughed her booming laugh. I couldn't help but smile in response. Nobody laughs like Miss Elva.

"Child, there's no other way to look, and you know that's the truth of it," Miss Elva said, climbing into the front seat of my car. "My mama was never caught dead without her face on and a good pair of earrings in. The only place I differ from her is that I don't like to be traipsing around in heels all the time. I prefer flats, in case I ever need to run."

I schooled my expression into not reacting to that as I tried to picture Miss Elva actually running anywhere. Or hurrying at all.

"Child, you go on and wipe that smirk off your face. I can hustle when I need to be hustling." Miss Elva swatted my arm and I laughed.

"I'm sure you can," I said, looking over my shoulder to pull away from the curb.

And screeched when my eyes landed on Rafe hovering outside my window.

"I'm not talking to you," I mouthed through the glass, and his expression grew more mutinous.

"Now, you go on and roll that window down. Rafe's got something he wants to say to you," Miss Elva scolded me.

I sighed, but I did what she said.

"What do you want?" I asked, glaring at the ghost.

Rafe pushed his pirate hat up on his head and threw his shoulders back.

"I would like to apologize for putting the love potion in the punch at the Valentine's Day party," Rafe said stiffly, looking past my shoulder at Miss Elva.

"You apologizing to me or to her, pirate?" I asked, pointing back at Miss Elva.

"You, I guess," Rafe spat out.

"Gee, thanks a lot. You're not forgiven," I said, and began to pull away. Rafe hurried to float next to the window.

"No, don't leave. I really didn't mean to do it. I was just blinded by rage at the thought of my lovemountain trying to find someone else to love," Rafe said desperately, his eyes huge and full of love for Miss Elva. I stopped the car and looked at her, then back at him.

"Is that what happened?"

"Yeah. This silly man thought I was making a love potion for me," Miss Elva scoffed in disbelief. "Like I need a potion to make men fall in love with me."

The woman had a point.

"Fine, Rafe, I'll forgive you. Pull something like that again, though, and Luna and I will send you back through the veil so fast you won't know what hit you," I warned, but Rafe had already exuberantly burst into the car and was hovering in the back seat behind us.

"I knew you wouldn't stay mad at me. Peasants never do."

"Great to have you back, Rafe, really great," I bit out as I pulled away from the curb.

Chapter Four

DOWNTOWN TEQUILA KEY is little more than a stretch of road where shops and restaurants clamor for space, and those with the most money secure the spots with the best ocean views. Space is at a premium here, and I was ecstatic to see that my best friend Beau's new restaurant looked like it would be open soon.

"Beau's going to make a killing at the new place," I said as I drove toward his other bar, the long-standing and wildly popular Lucky's Tiki Bar.

Perched a bit higher on a rocky outcropping at the end of the main street, Lucky's had become an institution in Tequila Key. A cross between kitschy and elegant, it served excellent seafood, a mean burger, and the best Mai-Tai in Tequila Key. Or in all the Keys, I would say if Beau were standing nearby to hear me.

I had my own parking spot, because I'm that cool. Or, you know, because Beau loves me that much. Or because I like to drink. It doesn't matter. I rarely drink to excess, as it's never good to get tipsy and try to go scuba diving or give readings the next day. But an after-work cocktail? Absolutely.

We followed the path of lit tiki torches up to the restaurant – a true hut-style building with a thatched roof – and breezed inside. A beautiful circular wooden bar dominated the room, and pufferfish lamps hung from the ceiling. Beau shook a cocktail mixer behind the bar and shot us a grin, but didn't break his conversation with a cute redhead at the bar.

I smiled. Women rarely picked up on the fact that Beau was gay. Guys never seemed to have a problem with figuring it out, though, and Beau was in and out of relationships as often as he mixed up cocktails. He even ran a not-so-secret afterhours gay club at the bar. The police looked the other way and Beau comped them their meals and drinks. It was a win for everyone.

"Loving the hair," Beau called, and I realized he hadn't seen the newest upgrade.

"Thanks," I said, twirling before sliding onto a seat at the bar. Miss Elva settled next to me and we both immediately scanned the room to see if anyone we knew was there.

"Nobody important," Miss Elva decided, then beamed at Beau. "Look at you, child, looking so cute I could 'bout eat you up."

"Glad you could make it back after the party debacle," Beau laughed.

Miss Elva winked at him. "I'm glad it turned out okay. Things could've taken a wild turn," she purred.

"Oh, the surveillance video is like watching a soft-core porn. I'm keeping that one in the safe in case I ever need to blackmail anyone in this town," Beau chuckled, but I had no doubt he was telling the truth.

"We may need to get tipsy and watch that some day," I said. Beau slid a mojito in front of me, already knowing what I would order.

"Do we need to discuss Theodore?" Beau asked, raising an eyebrow at Miss Elva.

"I don't see why we would need to do that," Miss Elva hummed and I looked between the two of them.

"Wait, what are you talking about? What did I miss?" I demanded.

Theodore Whittier was from one of the town's founding families. Rich, on the board of every committee, and with an opinion on everything – I pretty much considered him my nemesis.

"Well," Beau said, leaning in to whisper, "It seems… now, you can't quote me on this… but the impression that I received…"

"Child, don't even say it," Miss Elva warned, but her brown eyes were dancing with laughter.

"It seems that Mr. Whittier has a bit of crush on Miss Elva."

"What!" I screeched, inhaling a piece of mint through my straw and choking on it. I coughed as tears flooded my eyes. Miss Elva whacked me on the back, and I doubled over – in pain, this time.

"Yeesh, throttle back, woman," I murmured to Miss Elva, wiping my eyes.

"Sorry," Miss Elva said.

"Yes, seems he drank some of that potion and had nothing but the light of love in his eyes for Miss Thang over here." Beau gestured to Miss Elva, his face wreathed in delight. "It was quite possibly the best part of my night."

"No! I can't believe it. This is amazing," I breathed, just as Luna slid into a seat next to me.

"What's amazing?" Luna asked, smiling at Beau and Miss Elva.

"Theodore has a crush on Miss Elva," I gasped, still laughing.

It was Luna's turn to choke.

Once we'd all suitably recovered from that delightful bit of gossip, and after Beau had presented us with his famous guacamole and hand-cut tortilla chips, I focused on the reason we'd come.

"So, this Chadwick Harrington," I said, and Beau let out a low whistle as he breezed past us with drinks in his hand. "Am I the only one who doesn't know who this man is?"

Miss Elva rummaged in her purse – the depths of which may be unending, judging by what she has been seen to pull from it – and unearthed a copy of Newsweek. She handed it to me and I peered at the somewhat handsome – handsome in a sleazy way, mind you – man on the cover. The title beneath his beaming face said it all.

Is This the Most Hated Man in America?

With blond hair slicked back with some kind of gel, a tanned face, and unnaturally white teeth, Chadwick looked like a used car salesman on the prowl for his next victim.

"Pharma Boy screws millions by holding onto the patent for Alzheimer's cure," I said, reading further. Flipping the magazine open to the cover story, I scanned the first few paragraphs.

"Does he really have a cure?" I finally asked, looking up at Miss Elva and Luna.

Luna nodding, carefully selecting a chip and a miniscule amount of guacamole before responding.

"He does. And the FDA approved it and everything. However, his company is private, and they've jacked the prices up to some astronomical amount that only the richest of the rich can afford."

My mouth dropped open.

"But that's… that's…"

"Mathias says it's unconscionable," Luna said, referring to her current boyfriend, an urgent care doctor.

"Being an asshole? The work of the devil?" Miss Elva supplied, taking a sip of her beer.

"How does it even work?" I asked, still astounded that there was a cure for Alzheimer's.

"It reverses the neurological breakdown, or rebuilds the neurological pathways… something like that. Mathias tried to explain it to me. But, essentially, over a matter of months of taking this drug, the patient is restored to full mental acuity."

"So it's not like a vaccine or a one-and-done pill?" I asked.

Luna shook her head and took a sip of her margarita.

"Not in the slightest. Which is why what he is doing is so awful. The patient needs a significant amount of medication to rebuild these pathways or whatever, but he's jacked the price so high that it would easily take six figures or more to heal someone."

"That's insane," I breathed.

"And wrong. Just plain wrong. Work of the devil, I tell ya," Miss Elva intoned.

"So the shit hit the fan and he's come down here to dodge the press," I said, dipping my chip in the guac and then pausing for a moment to savor Beau's delicious recipe. He still wouldn't tell me the secret ingredients. One of these days I was going to sit on him and tickle him until he did.

"Pretty much. He's living large on his yacht and not worrying in the slightest about the damage he's causing by charging what he is. Though he's making a killing from those who can afford his cure."

"I'm sure. I just can't believe someone would do something like this. Alzheimer's is a huge problem!" I exclaimed and Miss Elva clucked her tongue at me, shaking her head at my naiveté.

"Child, the pharma industry's been like this for years. Cancer is big business. They've probably been sitting on a cure for ages, but nobody wants to reveal it because it will put all these big corporations out of business. In the meantime, people suffer and die because of the greed of big business. It's a nasty cycle and as a health practitioner myself, it makes me indignant."

Luna and I both regarded Miss Elva carefully.

"So you're a health practitioner now?" Luna asked sweetly.

"I am. Don't think I'm not. Just because my methods are a little more… out there, that doesn't mean I'm not improving people's health."

I pressed my lips together and raised my eyebrows at a beaming Beau, but said nothing.

"I see that look on your face, Althea," Miss Elva grumbled.

"I've got nothing to say on that matter. I've seen you work your magick before," I said, smiling at Miss Elva. It was true too – Miss Elva's methods may not be approved by the FDA, or by society in general, but I couldn't argue with the outcomes of her rituals.

"You'd better believe I know what I'm doing," Miss Elva said, rolling her eyes at where an uncharacteristically quiet Rafe hovered over her shoulder.

"Of course, Lovemountain. You're a warrior goddess whose power knows no bounds," Rafe said automatically, and I rolled my eyes.

"Why do you think someone like this wants his tarot cards read?" I asked, instead of commenting on Rafe's over-the-top comment.

"My thoughts? He's bored," Luna said, shrugging one shoulder.

"Wait, you're going to read for this guy?" Beau asked, stopping back to catch up on the story. I filled him in quickly and he shook his head at me.

"Girl, can you put something in his drink? One of Miss Elva's potions? Maybe she could make a nice guy potion."

"Hmmm," Miss Elva said immediately, leaning back to cross her arms across her formidable chest. "I'd need a little time, but I'm thinking I could mix something up."

"No, please, I'm not doing anything like that. You all know how un-stealthy I am. I'll just trip and spill it on someone or put it in the wrong drink."

"She's absolutely right. Though I'm thinking maybe one of us should go with her. I'm not sure I like her going on this boat by herself."

We all paused at that.

"I'll go. Luna needs to keep the store up," Miss Elva decided.

And just like that, I had an escort.

Chapter Five

I CAN'T SAY I slept all that well. When I'd gotten home from Lucky's, I'd spent far too long researching Chadwick Harrington. And the more dirt I unearthed on him, the more I was convinced that he was what we would call NOT A GOOD PERSON.

It hadn't helped that Cash had chosen last night to call and ask if he could come see me today. I had to stutter and stall until he finally grew exasperated with me.

"It's because you're with Trace now, isn't it?"

"No, I haven't seen him. Much like I haven't seen you. I'm pretty much convinced it's best that I swear off all men."

Cash hadn't liked that either, but it had thrown him off the scent of what I was really doing today. Because I was more than certain that if I told him that I was giving a private reading to the most hated man in America, he'd pretty much have a fit.

I shook my head and tucked a curl behind my ear

before automatically reaching down to toss the ball for Hank. I was enjoying my lazy morning on my back porch, sipping coffee and contemplating life before Miss Elva arrived to go with me to the boat. I mean, yacht.

Personally, I felt that maybe swearing off all men for a while was a sound idea. So what if Cash and Trace both made my skin flush and made me have thoughts that would embarrass the proper women of Port Atticus? As an adult, I prided myself on having spectacular impulse control.

I glanced down at the second half-eaten donut in my hand.

Scratch that. I was so screwed.

Hank's ecstatic barks announced Miss Elva's arrival and I called out to her from where I sat.

"Out back!"

"It is a nice morning for it, isn't it," Miss Elva said as she came through the sliding glass doors, a dancing Hank on her heels. Today's caftan was deep purple – the color of royalty – and an intricate amethyst crystal headband was wound through the hair at the crown of her head.

"Not so humid today," I agreed, pointing to a cup of coffee I'd already poured for her. It was in keeping with Miss Elva's perverse nature to drink hot coffee all year round, irrespective of the weather.

"Donuts?"

"I was in a mood." I shrugged and tossed the ball for Hank again.

"I like this mood," Miss Elva decided as she poked around in the box before pulling out a simple glazed donut.

Say what you will about donuts – there is nothing

better than a perfectly round glazed donut. I don't care how much frosting and cinnamon and sprinkles other donuts have. I'm a purist when it comes to my pastries.

"You look subdued today," Miss Elva said, glancing over my simple black maxi dress and my tamed hair. I'd pulled my riot of curls back into a poufy ponytail at the nape of my neck and had hung a simple quartz pendant from my neck.

"I'm feeling subdued. I didn't sleep well and I'm not looking forward to this. I have a bad feeling about today," I admitted, and took another bite of my donut. I mean, if I was swearing off men, why should I care about a few extra pounds?

"Child, I don't feel good about it either. But if he's going to hang out down here for a while, it's best we get an idea of what we're dealing with. And if anything, we can give Chief Thomas a little background info."

Chief Thomas was the local sheriff, who had taken over from a particularly nasty sheriff who had wanted to kill me. You know, life as usual over here in Tequila Key.

"I find it amusing that we take it upon ourselves to be the ones to check out the nefarious characters who swing through Tequila Key. I mean, shouldn't that be left to the professionals?" I asked, and Miss Elva met my eyes for a beat.

Then we both laughed.

"Please, honey, like we keep our noses out of anything that goes on around here. Think that Veronica woman will be there?"

"Victoria, and yes, I think she's the one picking us up."

As I said the words, my doorbell rang, sending Hank into a frenzy.

"Let's do this," I said and stood up, walking to the drawer where I kept Hank's toys. I rotated them out, so he felt like he constantly got a "new" toy.

"Ohhhh, it's a banana today!" I said, holding a large yellow stuffed banana above my head and squeaking it dramatically. Hank whipped his little body in circles at my feet and I tossed it across the room, sending him slipping and sliding over the wood floors after it.

"After you," I murmured, allowing Miss Elva to open the door. I wanted to get a read on Victoria's face when she saw Miss Elva.

I wasn't disappointed.

Victoria's eyebrows rose to her hairline as she took in the full force that was Miss Elva, then she looked past her to meet my eyes.

"Is she…" Victoria wasn't sure how to phrase the question.

"Coming with me? Yes, she works with me. It's best to have two people for a party," I said smoothly, stepping out onto the porch and locking my door. We all stood there awkwardly for a moment while Victoria digested the information.

"I'm one of the best in the business, honey, so I hope you're not being insulting right now," Miss Elva snapped out at Victoria's silence.

The uptight woman jumped. "No, of course not. Please, this way," Victoria said, gesturing to where a black town car idled at the curb. Victoria seemed to have figured out that leather didn't work in this heat, as today she wore another fitted pencil skirt, but in a more forgiving material. Her hair was once again pulled back so tightly that I wondered if it literally sprang out of the bun when she pulled the ties out at night. Or maybe she slept with it in a bun. Maybe she was always uptight?

Miss Elva rolled her eyes at me behind Victoria's back and I grinned at her as we reached the car and slipped into the cool interior. Victoria took the passenger seat and didn't glance back at us once as we rode in silence through the town. Miss Elva slid a glance at me and then tossed a thought into my head.

Doesn't seem like we're going to a party.

Not in the slightest, I threw back at her.

Good thing I'm packing.

My eyes bulged at that one, but I kept my mouth shut. One of the delightful things about having a voodoo priestess with magickal powers for a friend is that we could send our thoughts into each other's minds when necessary. It takes some work, but once mastered, it's an invaluable skill.

So far we'd just used it to make comments on drunk tourists at the tiki bar, but you know, in case of an emergency it would be highly useful.

We passed the docks where the fishermen and the dive boats regularly tied up, and my eyes automatically went to where Trace's boat was usually docked. His slip was empty, so I could only assume he was out with his dive clients today. I missed diving. And I missed him, if I was being truly honest. One of these days, one of us was going to have to be the adult and address what had happened at the party so we could go back to being friends.

Or something more.

The thought of something more with Trace wasn't entirely unappealing, which just shows why I needed to swear off men altogether for a while. Clearly, I wasn't capable of making sound decisions at the moment.

"Nice boat," Miss Elva commented, and I shook myself from my thoughts and checked out the yacht docked at the private country club landing.

"Yacht," I mouthed to Miss Elva as Victoria turned around and said the same thing.

Miss Elva winked at me.

"Nice yacht," Miss Elva said smoothly.

"Yes, it's brand new. There's a pool, two kitchens, a hot tub, a helicopter landing pad, ten rooms, and room for a crew of thirty. And outfitted with the latest technology, naturally," Victoria rattled off as if she were reading from a brochure.

"Naturally," Miss Elva nodded, not a wisp of sarcasm in her voice.

"Isn't it a little early for a party?" I asked as the car rolled to a stop. It was barely noon and here we were for a yacht party.

"It's always a party on the yacht," Victoria said scathingly – but I got the distinct impression her ire wasn't directed at me this time.

"Naturally," I said, allowing sarcasm to drip from my words. Miss Elva was showing more restraint than me.

Victoria ignored my comment and got out of the car, not bothering to open our doors for us. We both exited the vehicle and stood by the gate to the dock, standing quietly as Victoria ignored us and punched in the code for the gate while the town car quietly pulled away.

"You'll be expected to take your shoes off, and turn off your cell phones. No pictures, of course. As you are probably aware, Mr. Harrington is in high demand at the moment and we can't have anything being leaked to the press. I'll also have you sign a standard non-disclosure agreement once we are on the yacht. Can't be too careful, of course," Victoria said as she tripped up the dock to where a uniformed security guard stood by the floating plank that connected the dock to the yacht.

I had anticipated the bit about the phones and had left mine at home, but hadn't expected the NDA. It didn't really matter to me one way or the other. Confidentiality is a given in my line of work. I wouldn't have repeat customers if I went and blabbed everyone's business all over town.

"I didn't bring my phone," I said to Victoria as we approached the guard. Victoria shrugged nonchalantly.

"The guard will do a pat-down either way. See you shortly," she trilled and waved to the guard before disappearing into the bowels of the boat. I raised an eyebrow at the guard and smiled.

He didn't smile back.

"Mmmhmm, honey child, you can pat me down all you want," Miss Elva cooed. I saw the guard's eyes widen slightly and had to choke back a laugh.

We were ushered quickly on board into a dark hallway, and pushed into a small room that held one other guard, a small desk, and a couple of chairs. I assumed this was their "intake" room, so to speak.

"Ma'am, I'll have to ask you to put your hands in the air while I pat you down. And please hand over your purse." I was surprised to see that Miss Elva had brought only a small clutch today. She'd clearly anticipated the same thing I had, and wasn't willing to subject her larger satchel to a search.

Miss Elva winked at the guard, causing a faint blush to tinge his cheeks as he patted her down. In moments, he did the same to me. I admired that he kept his cool around Miss Elva and he treated us both in a professional manner, which I was thankful for. I didn't want to have to get into it with someone taking liberties on a pat-down before we'd even gotten to the main point of our visit.

"You ladies are free to go after you sign the NDA," the guard said brusquely, pointing to the desk where a clipboard sat with a contract on it. I picked it up and scanned it, and was relieved to find that it was a boilerplate NDA contract. You never know what people will try to slip into contracts, so I took my time reading any extra clauses.

"Fairly standard," I said to Miss Elva and she nodded. But I noticed that when it was her turn to sign, she took her time to read it too.

Miss Elva is nobody's fool.

"You're all set. Follow the hallway to the stairs and head to the main deck," the first guard instructed, his eyebrows raising again as Miss Elva blew him a kiss on the way out the door. I shot him a quick smile and the corner of his mouth quirked a bit before his face settled back into granite.

"Ready to rub elbows with the rich and famous?" Miss

Elva said over her shoulder as we approached the stairs at the end of a long – very long – hallway.

"I suppose. If we must," I grumbled, making Miss Elva throw back her head and hoot out her booming laugh.

Which was exactly what caused the party on the top deck to come to a grinding halt when we emerged from below-decks.

Chapter Six

"THIS IS A PARTY?" Miss Elva whispered over her shoulder to me. I shrugged. Who was I to say how the rich and famous should have fun? But from what I could see, it looked like everyone was zoned out – on drugs or on sheer boredom – and nobody was smiling. Scads of half-naked women pouted around the pool, arranging themselves artfully in their chaise lounges. A few men in bright polo shirts with popped collars and khaki shorts sprawled near a low table loaded with tequila bottles and a dice cup. A man, presumably a DJ, sat behind turntables but looked to be just picking songs on his laptop. The only person in the room smiling was the man I recognized immediately as Chadwick Harrington.

"Finally! My surprise has arrived," Chadwick said, getting up from the table of men and clapping his hands. Miss Elva's laugh had already drawn all eyes to us, but now the women pouted further and squirmed in their chairs. I wanted to roll my eyes at them. They couldn't possibly consider us their competition, I thought. A quick scan of their thoughts revealed that we had indeed been sized up as a potential threat and dismissed, which, in turn, made me angry.

I never said I don't have a contradictory nature.

"Someone should tell those girls to stop posing and lighten up and have some fun. That's why the men are all over here playing dice and not over there chatting them up," Miss Elva murmured knowingly to me. "Say what you will about having a perfect body and all – men want someone they can have fun with outside the bedroom, too."

Since I was far from having a perfect body, all I could do was concede her point that men like girls who know how to have fun. I mean, that's probably why I was juggling both Trace and Cash, right? I didn't have time to think too deeply about it as Chadwick finally reached us.

"Ladies, it's a delight to have you here," Chadwick said, his white smile blinding as he held out his hand to us. He didn't blink at the fact that there were two of us, so I had to assume Victoria, who was sipping a seltzer bottle at the bar, had briefed him. Judging by the angry expression on her face, I concluded that she had, and that her work must be done for the day. I wondered again in what capacity she worked for Chadwick.

"Mr. Harrington, I'm Althea Rose. I thought it would be best to bring backup as I had no idea how large your party would be and how many people would be interested in having readings done. I thought it might be more efficient to bring a second along. This is the eminently qualified Miss Elva," I said, introducing him to Miss Elva.

Chadwick smiled and shook her hand before turning with a sweep of his hand to where the men sat.

"Elva, Althea, please, join us."

"That's Miss Elva to you, and, well, to just about everyone," Miss Elva said, booming out her big laugh again. I caught the flash of anger that crossed Chadwick's face before he smiled again. There's the real Chadwick, I thought.

"Of course. My apologies."

"No need to apologize, sweetheart, just clarifying is all. Now, tell me, how does it feel to own a big ol' boat like this?" Miss Elva said, smoothing over the moment quickly.

"Yacht," Chadwick said automatically, and I bit back a smile as the men stood and pulled chairs out for us.

Chadwick warmed to Miss Elva, going on about all the great things about the boat, while I sized up the two men who stood before me. One, tanned and tall with silver glasses shading his eyes, looked to be just as wealthy as Chadwick, what with the Rolex on his wrist and the Italian leather shoes. I briefly wondered how come he was allowed to wear shoes, then turned to scan the short, squat man with a dark mustache and an eager-to-please look on his face.

Chadwick and expensive-watch-man were the rich ones, and the stuffed sausage was the muscle, I estimated quickly.

"Ladies, this is Nathaniel Amaigo, my best friend," Chadwick said with an easy smile as he introduced us to the Rolex-wearing man. Nathaniel smiled charmingly at us both, and shook our hands. I liked that he didn't try to squeeze my hand too hard. I hated when men tried to assert their dominance with an overly strong handshake. Turning expectantly to the squat man, I held out my hand.

"Oh, and that's Nico," Chadwick said with a little wave, dismissing the man. I watched irritation flash in Nico's eyes before he smiled at both of us.

"Such beauty to join us on such a fine day," Nico said, his accent thick with the harder edge of Brooklyn streets.

"It really is a delightful day, isn't it?" Miss Elva said, taking a seat and smiling brightly at Nico. I still wondered where she was packing – or maybe what she was packing? Whatever she was carrying, if anything, had gotten past the security guards.

"The breeze sure do make it the perfect day, don't it?" Nico guffawed and slapped his hand on his knee. I liked him already, even though I knew he was the hired muscle – I think partly because I could tell his uncouth nature set Chadwick's jaw on edge.

"Something to drink for you ladies?" A butler had appeared soundlessly at Chadwick's side.

"I'll have a soda water with a lime," I said.

"Aw, that's no fun," Nico exclaimed. "How about a martini?"

"I can't give a clear reading if I've been drinking," I explained gently.

Nico put his hand to his mustache, nodding seriously. "Yeah, don't that just make sense though? You need to be all clearheaded to get those psychic images. I read all about it. My mother goes to her psychic monthly, Lord help us all. I never hear the end of the impending doom in my life if I don't quit my job and get married, you know?" Nico slapped his hand on his leg and laughed again.

"I'm pretty sure she's just trying to marry you off so you'll give her grandchildren," Nathaniel said with a small smile.

"That's not the life for me. She's got some grandchildren already. You'd think she'd be happy by now." Nico shook his head.

"Mothers are never happy until you settle down and have kids," Chadwick said, and I turned my attention to him.

"Do you have children?"

"Shouldn't you know? You're the psychic," Chadwick parried, and I realized just what type of reading this was going to be.

See, here's the thing with being psychic – a lot of people who come to me are skeptics. To which I say, why even come then? They just spend the whole reading challenging me or trying to get me to prove myself. It can be exhausting and, frankly, insulting.

"You don't have any kids, or you wouldn't be on this here yacht," Miss Elva laughed, "though I'm surprised your wife let you come down here without her."

Chadwick straightened and I saw Nathaniel's lips press tightly together.

"How do you know she isn't here?"

Miss Elva nodded her head toward the bevy of half-naked women.

"Unless she's one of them, I can't imagine most wives would be happy with this set-up."

"Good thing you signed an NDA," Chadwick bit out and I realized we were getting off on the wrong foot.

"Chadwick, our job isn't to judge – anything. If you

only knew the amount of people and problems we encounter on a daily basis – frankly, it's exhausting. So, trust me when I say, your personal matters are your own. Miss Elva was making an observation, but she certainly wasn't judging."

"Judge not, lest ye be judged," Miss Elva concurred.

Chadwick relaxed and nodded as our drinks were set on the table in front of us.

"So how does this work? Do you just throw some cards down and tell us our future?"

"Well, typically I'd see if you have particular questions you'd like answered," I explained as I pulled my tarot cards out – Nico coming to alert as I reached my hand in my bag – and set the cards on the table. "But I can also do an overall reading for the near future, that kind of thing."

A brunette in a strip of red cloth that constituted a bikini wandered over and perched on the side of the couch to wrap her arm around Chadwick's shoulder.

"Baby, can I watch?"

"No, this is for the men," Chadwick said, his handsome face creasing with annoyance as he all but shoved her off of him. The girl stomped off, her considerable assets jiggling on the way, and the men all watched her appreciatively.

"You sure do like making her mad, boss," Nico said, confirming that his relationship to Chadwick was also a paid one.

"It's fun to make it up to her," Chadwick said fondly, and I tried to not let any emotion slip over my face. Oddly enough, I felt like Nathaniel seemed to be projecting a similar level of disgust, and I wondered if he had a thing for the brunette as well.

"Who would like to start?" I asked, deciding to steer the conversation away from the bikini and the very obvious affair Chadwick was conducting. For all I knew, the wife knew about it. Who's to say? Maybe they had an open marriage.

"That's all you, bossman," Nico said, pulling a gold chain with a cross dangling from it from beneath his t-shirt. "I'm Catholic."

"And what does that have to do with tarot?" Miss Elva asked, tilting her head at him in question.

"Um, well, isn't it, you know, black magic?" Nico asked, tugging nervously on his mustache.

Miss Elva and I looked at each other before rolling our eyes.

"What? I'm just saying…" Nico trailed off and shrugged.

"It's not black magic. We never seek to harm, we only seek to help," I said gently, smiling at Nico to soften my words. "And your mother doesn't seem to have a problem with seeing a psychic, you know."

"I suppose that's nice then. But I'm still not doing it." Nico shrugged and got up to wander to the bar, where he procured a Miller High Life.

"Gentlemen?" I asked, looking between Nathaniel and Chadwick.

"I'll start," Nathaniel said. Chadwick was surprised but I could see tension ease from his shoulders. It always surprised me when seemingly intelligent people were spooked by what I did for a living. If only they knew what

I could do – or, really, what Miss Elva was capable of – getting a tarot card reading would be at the bottom of the list of things that would worry them.

"Show me the future, pretty lady," Nathaniel said, throwing me a wink.

So I did.

Chapter Seven

TAROT CARDS ARE finicky at best and indecisive at their worst. They never will say 'this is one hundred percent what lies in the future.' I liken tarot to the wizened old man the trodden-down warrior meets upon his path who offers invaluable wisdom and guidance. For me, tarot is a serious business – for others it's nothing but a fun party trick.

Irrespective of who sits on the other side of the table from me, I always take my business seriously.

That's just ethics.

When Nathaniel flashed me a wink, I knew that everything he was going to say to me was a lie. I just didn't know what his game was yet.

"Is there anything particular you'd like to focus on in today's reading?" I asked primly as I shuffled the deck and handed the stack of weathered tarot cards to him. He looked down at them in his palm for a moment.

"See if he's ever going to settle down, or if he's going to George Clooney it the rest of his life," Chadwick laughed.

"George Clooney did get married. To that gorgeous lawyer. He just waited till he found himself some brains and beauty," Miss Elva pointed out.

"Yeah, like that ever happens," Chadwick said, crossing his arms over his chest and rolling his eyes.

Was this guy a teenager? How had he become the head of one of the most elite and illustrious private pharma companies in the nation?

"I know plenty of beautiful and smart women," I said to Chadwick, but took the bite out of my tone with a smile.

"Yeah, you're looking at two of them right here," Miss Elva said, leaning back and putting a hand on her hip.

Even Chadwick didn't dare to contradict Miss Elva, so he just nodded and waved at me to proceed.

I brought my focus back to the man who sat across from me. "Is that what you'd like to know about today? Love?" I asked Nathaniel.

His gaze flashed to the woman in the red bikini, who was currently using a selfie stick to get a perfect angle on her bikini shot. His eyes met mine.

"Love is for fools and the weak," Nathaniel said softly. "I'd like to know how my career path looks."

Years of reading tarot had taught me to school my expression, so I didn't raise an eyebrow at what Nathaniel said. But if I were a gambling person, I'd bet money that he very much did believe in love.

"Depends on what type of love you're talking 'bout, honey," Miss Elva laughed. "In my mind, there's all kinds. Sometimes just lasting for a couple hours, too."

Chadwick laughed and raised a curled fist into the air. Miss Elva cocked her head at it in confusion.

"You fist-bumping me, child?"

"Um, er, no?" Chadwick said, lowering his fist into his lap. Again I saw the flash of anger behind his eyes. I hoped Miss Elva wouldn't push him too far, and I shot her a quick warning glance.

"Different generations, honey. I wasn't raised on fist-bumping like you kids were," Miss Elva said smoothly, and I saw the line on Chadwick's forehead smooth out.

"Shuffle the cards and when you feel ready, divide them into three piles," I directed Nathaniel. As he did so, I opened my mind to focus on his energy.

And was met with a blank wall.

Now, I'm not saying I'm the most gifted psychic in the world – that would be my mother, the infamous Abigail Rose – but I'm pretty damn good at what I do. And when I meet a wall of silence when reading someone's mental signature, it means one of two things – either he's mentally deficient or he's blocking me.

Since Nathaniel didn't strike me as being deficient, I had to assume the opposite was true. That he was indeed very, very smart – and he knew how to block a mental probe.

Something to think about for later, I thought as I began flipping cards over and laying them out on the table.

"Oh, the death card!" Chadwick exclaimed and I shook my head at him, smiling a little.

"Not what you think it means," I said quickly.

"What does it mean, then?" Chadwick said, leaning in.

"When you read cards, you take a look at the whole picture," I explained, pointing to where the death card lay in the formation. "For example, the three of cups is reversed in this position, which would typically mean 'three's a crowd.' So as a whole, when we read the spread and focus on the question that was posed in regards to career paths, I'd say the death card symbolizes a fairly sudden – and quite significant – change of directions is in your near future."

Nathaniel nodded solemnly at the words, but did not register surprise. In fact, the only surprised person at the table was Chadwick.

"No way would you leave your security business. That doesn't make sense," Chadwick exclaimed. "You're one of the best computer geeks in the industry."

Nathaniel shrugged.

"Maybe I'm getting burned out."

"So you take a vacation. Shit, take six months off. You don't just stop what you love doing," Chadwick said and I was surprised at the depth of his insight. You'd think that a pharma guy who was currently lounging on a boat – a *yacht* – miles away from the fallout of the publicity shit-storm he'd inflicted upon his company would be telling his friend to live the high life and never work again.

"Do you love what you do?" Miss Elva asked.

Nathaniel shrugged again and then leaned back to stretch, an easy smile on his face. I didn't believe his ease for a moment. The minute I'd told him he would be changing paths, I'd sensed he'd gone on high alert.

"I like running my company. But perhaps it is time for a change. I just haven't figured out what that change is yet." Nathaniel shrugged.

"Ah, you'll change your mind. You make too much damn money to just walk away from everything you've built." Chadwick brushed Nathaniel's words aside. "What about the ladies? Do you see lots of ladies in there for him? He's been kind of a drag lately."

Knowing that Nathaniel had already specifically requested we not read about his love life, I cast my eyes down at the cards, then over at Chadwick.

"Unfortunately, that wasn't factored into this spread as it was a career-focused reading."

I didn't say what I saw.

There definitely was a love in Nathaniel's life.

Chapter Eight

"THAT WAS BORING," Chadwick said, rolling his eyes. "Let's do mine." Both Victoria and the butler wandered over at his words and I wondered if their intrusiveness would anger Chadwick.

It didn't surprise me when he barely registered their presence. Some rich people are like that with their help – they fade into the background as part of the ebb and flow of what makes their daily existence possible.

Nathaniel held up a slim cigar. "Ladies, do you mind if I smoke?"

Ever the polite one, he is, I thought, and nodded my assent.

The sticky-sweet acrid smell of a very expensive cigar soon surrounded us, while Chadwick shuffled the cards.

"Well, I don't need to know about love," Chadwick snickered as he glanced over at Red Bikini.

"Because you've found the love of your life," I said easily, referencing his wife, not Red Bikini.

"I don't think I hold with all that nonsense," Chadwick

said, secure in his conviction that he had enough money and power to do and say what he wanted.

Then why get married? It was on the tip of my tongue to ask, but I held back. It wasn't hard to scan Chadwick's thoughts. Unlike Nathaniel, he was a clear projector, and I picked up on the fact that not only was he disinterested in his wife, but Red Bikini was beginning to bore him as well. I wondered if any of them knew Victoria had professed her love to Chadwick. For some reason, the thought didn't surprise me when I plucked it from Chadwick's mind. Though nothing had indicated that Victoria had any interest in Chadwick outside of a professional capacity, I'd caught an image of her unbuttoning her shirt in front of Chadwick's desk.

So women were his playthings, I quickly summed up, and smiled brightly at Chadwick.

"So, career then?"

"Nah, I think we all know my career is solid," Chadwick guffawed loudly, looking around as everyone laughed right along with him.

Was it though? It seemed extra cocky of him to say such a thing when his company was in crisis mode.

"Just give me an overall read of this coming year. Like… what do I have to be worried about? Any surprise babies? That kind of thing." Chadwick's teeth flashed white in his tanned face. Victoria's hand tightened on the back of the couch at his question.

I studied the cards laid before me. I wasn't surprised to see the potential for a child – I mean, he was sleeping with everyone he could – but I was surprised to see just how much of a warning the cards were trying to give me.

Frankly, I don't think I'd seen a more tense layout since… well, since Luna's boyfriend had been found with anchors attached to his ankles.

"What? Am I going to die or something?" Chadwick laughed, but the sound fell flat.

"We're all going to die," I said, my automatic response to that question.

"So… what then?"

"Well, funny you should mention children," I decided to start with that and Chadwick's eyebrows rose to his forehead.

"You're shitting me."

"I'm saying that the cards see a potential for a child. That doesn't mean it *will* happen. But, I guess what I'm saying is that if you want one, there's an opportunity for it. But…"

"But?" Chadwick asked, his index finger tapping on his knee.

"The way I'm interpreting this spread is that this is a big warning."

"A warning how? About who I sleep with?" Chadwick said, leaning forward to study the cards in front of me, as if he had any idea what they actually meant.

"A warning to trust no one," I said softly, calling it as I saw it.

"In what respect?" Chadwick said, his voice becoming angry.

"Tread carefully this year and trust no one," I said again, refusing to look at any of the people clustered around Chadwick, nor at the women sunning themselves by the pool. I had just entered dangerous territory. Nico's hand by his side, where he very obviously was carrying a weapon, reminded me again just whom I was dealing with.

"I'd say our work here is done," Miss Elva said smoothly, interrupting the silence. "Unless anyone else wants a reading?"

"You can't just leave," Chadwick said, interrupting her and facing me. "Tell me who I can't trust."

"It doesn't work like that," I began, and Chadwick swept all of my cards onto the floor.

"Hey!" I said. That was my favorite deck of tarot cards.

"Tell me who." Chadwick gritted his teeth.

"I wish I knew the answer to that," I said evenly, holding his gaze. It was true, too. I really did wish I knew.

The problem was that Chadwick had surrounded himself with people who were there for his money – not because they liked him. He'd built a false world for himself, so there was no way for me to pick just one person he couldn't trust. Money blinds people sometimes. As Oprah once said, "Everyone wants to ride with you in the limo, but what you want is someone who will take the bus with you when the limo breaks down."

"You were paid a lot of money for your services," Chadwick said, anger making him uglier than I already thought he was.

"I was paid to give you an honest reading. I'm not a Magic 8-Ball that you can shake and get all the answers you need. You're a businessman, you run a very big company; perhaps you should listen to your gut and pay attention to who you can and can't trust," I said, bending to gather my cards.

Chadwick leaned over me and began to hyperventilate at my words. "You're implying it's my job to figure this out, even though that's what I paid you for?"

"She's not implying." Miss Elva stood. "She's telling you that you need to watch your back. She can't hold your hand for you in this house of cards you've built for yourself. You're going to have to find your own way out. Or not. That's not our problem. Or our job."

Pharma Boy gave one look to Nico, and we found ourselves back on the dock faster than you can say "I'm vacationing on the yacht this summer."

Nico paused before he turned back to the boat.

"You really think he's got to watch his back?"

I read the stress in Nico's eyes; it was his job to protect Chadwick. He didn't have to like him, but this was someone who took his job seriously.

"I'd say so. I think he can't trust anyone. And you can't tell me you're surprised by that."

Nico shook his head sadly, his eyes trailing up to the yacht where we could hear Chadwick yelling.

"No, I'm not surprised in the least."

Chapter Nine

"DID YOU CATCH that bit about Victoria?" I asked Miss Elva after the car dropped us off in front of Lucky's Tiki bar. My heart was beating a little faster than normal, so I forced myself to take deep, even breaths.

"What – that the uptight hussy has the hots for her bossman? Yeah, I read that loud and clear," Miss Elva said, smoothing her hands down her caftan.

"Did you read that she's pregnant?" I asked Miss Elva, tilting my head at her in question.

"Sho did, child. Did you see the color drain from her face when you mentioned that? I swear, you should win an Oscar for how you didn't give that away. I was about ready to start pointing fingers and naming names."

"Man, did I ever want to look at her. But I couldn't." I ran a hand through my hair. "Last thing we needed was a cat-fight between Red Bikini and Victoria."

Silence hung between us for a moment.

"Victoria would take her," Miss Elva decided.

"Totally would," I agreed.

"That steward was weird," Miss Elva said.

"Steward? Oh, the butler? Yeah, he pretty much hated every second of his job." I agreed. The steward had been a tiny man with mean, beady-looking bird eyes.

"Shannon was his name. I'd be mad if my name was Shannon," Miss Elva said.

"Isn't that a girl's name?" I asked as we walked past the tiki torches lining the path to the door.

"Who cares if it's a girl's name or a boy's name? The only Shannons I've ever known are awful people," Miss Elva said, and sniffed.

Well then, I thought, and made a mental note to ask her sometime what Shannon had wronged her.

"That boat was not fun. You always think the rich and famous are going to be having these wild, crazy parties, but that was just—" I held my hand in front of my face and pretended to yawn.

"Total snoozefest," Miss Elva agreed as we opened the door to Lucky's. "If I had all that money, you'd know I'd be having a non-stop party. Good food, good music, and great people. None of this 'too snooty to say hello' type crap you get from those sticks sitting by the pool."

"Maybe they don't come alive until after dark," I said, then froze when I saw who was sitting at the bar.

"Move it, Althea. It's not like you haven't been all over this man before," Miss Elva hissed at me. I swear I felt a blush creep up my body as I thought about the last time Trace's hands had been all over my body.

Granted, it had been fueled by a love spell, but the body remembers what it wants.

Trace's smile was tentative, but I could read the happiness in his eyes when he looked at me. He looked gorgeous, as usual, and I sighed – I was certain that I was a rumpled disheveled mess. I resisted the urge to check my hair or smooth my dress, and smiled back at him.

Trace – all lean muscles, tanned skin, and streaky blond hair pulled into a nub at his neck – was the epitome of surfer casual. As a dive master, he ran his own dive operation, which was how he and I had become best friends. I'd linked up with him to go diving for my photography, and we'd fallen into an easy pattern of catching a few early-morning fun dives a week before he took clients out. Over time, a strong friendship had developed. And it wasn't until my sort-of boyfriend, Cash, had entered the picture that Trace had expressed an interest in me.

That had certainly added a new level of tension to our time spent alone on the dive boat. I hadn't seen Trace since the disastrous Valentine's Day party a few weeks ago, and I felt heat lick low in my stomach as my eyes met his.

"I was hoping I'd see you here," Trace said, pulling out the stools next to him. I waited to see if Miss Elva would sit next to him, but she chose one seat over. I made a mental note to smack her later.

"Were you? You could've just called me if you wanted to see me," I said lightly, as I slid onto the stool. A new bartender was working the bar today, and I wondered if Beau was busy supervising the finishing touches on his new high-end seafood restaurant at the other end of the strip.

"No need to get snarky. I've been busy," Trace said, bumping his knee against mine in admonishment.

"It wasn't snarky, it was just honesty. You know how

to find me if you want to see me," I pointed out, smiling at the bartender as he approached.

"Well, yes, I do. And, hey, look! I found you!" Trace said, his eyes wide with exaggeration. I couldn't decide if I wanted to smack or kiss the smile off his face, so I just rolled my eyes and looked at the bartender.

"I'll have a mojito, please, and the cheeseburger special." I had the rest of the day off now, I could have a cocktail.

"I'll have the same, but make mine a Corona." Miss Elva nodded at the bartender and then shifted to look at us.

"Y'all need to stop bickering and figure out if you're going to do the bedroom boogie-woogie or not," Miss Elva said.

Did I say I wanted to smack her later? I was now envisioning throwing her off a boat in the middle of the night with cement boots.

Burying my face in my hands, I just shook my head and laughed. There was literally no way for me to respond to that without getting myself in trouble.

"What do you say, Althea? Want to dance?" Trace's voice had a husky little timbre to it that made all my nerve endings go on alert. I kept my face buried in my hands for another moment.

"I'm fairly certain you've already got a dance partner," I finally said, raising my face to meet Trace's eyes. He shrugged, making the tattoos winding up his arms ripple.

"I had a dance partner. I no longer do."

Huh, that was new. Last I'd seen him, he'd had some skinny vacuous blonde hanging all over him at the Valentine's Day party. It was the type he typically attracted, and it seemed like every couple months another ditsy bikini-clad girl would rotate through his arms.

"I'm sure you'll find another dance partner soon enough. It's not all that difficult for you," I pointed out, reaching for the mojito as the bartender slid it across the bar to me. The cool mint soothed my burning throat.

"As I already asked – you want to dance?"

I fell silent as I considered where this was coming from. If he really wanted to date me, he should have called me and asked me out. Or come to my house like he so often did, to have a beer and throw the ball for Hank. To see me by happenstance and then declare that he wanted to date just didn't sit well with me.

"No thanks," I said, snagging a crispy French fry from the plate that the bartender set in front of me.

"Althea Rose, that is no way to treat a man who is declaring his love for you," Miss Elva admonished. Trace and I both sat back in our stools at that.

"I wasn't declaring my love," Trace sputtered.

"He wasn't… it wasn't…" I trailed off and narrowed my eyes at Trace. "You don't love me?"

"Well, of course I love you, you're one of my best friends," Trace said, demonstrating that by stealing a fry from my plate, "But like, I wasn't, you know, dropping down on bended knee or anything either."

"Well, maybe until you can consider doing that, you shouldn't be sniffing around her," Miss Elva said, and I jerked my gaze over to her.

"Miss Elva! Jeez, no. Just no. Nobody's said anything about wanting to get married – least of all me. Just… can we not do this? It's already been a tough day. I'd like to eat my cheeseburger in peace."

Trace glared at Miss Elva but she met his look head on. As any smart person would, Trace backed down and shifted his gaze back to me.

"What happened today? What's wrong?"

"Nothing's wrong, I guess. I just can't shake the feeling that there are some bad dudes out on that yacht." I quickly filled Trace in on our day. He leaned back in his chair, crossing his arms over his chest as he thought about it.

"Frankly, I can't say I really care if anything happens to him. He's a bad person."

Trace had a point. Chadwick was an awful person – and it wasn't on me to protect him or, frankly, even worry about what happened to him. I mean, I didn't wish any harm on him. I just wasn't going to lose any sleep over Chadwick and his house of lies.

"The man has a point," Miss Elva said, raising her cheeseburger in agreement.

"Oh, now you like him?" I grumbled.

"Miss Elva's always liked me. But she also likes to put me in my place," Trace said cheerfully, the peace restored once again.

Between them, at least. Because after that little bomb Trace just dropped on me, I was feeling anything but peaceful.

Chapter Ten

YOU'D BE CORRECT in assuming I had trouble sleeping that night. I mean, why sleep when I could lie awake imagining what my life would be like if I dated Trace? Or if I decided to work things out with Cash? How much of myself would I have to compromise in a relationship? Was it worth it? What did I really want?

Needless to say, the loud banging at my door just past six in the morning – when I'd finally drifted off just after four – was not welcome.

Hank went ballistic, shooting off my bed in a twenty-pound ball of ferociousness as he barreled down the stairs and barked at the front door. Grimacing, I glanced at the time on my clock and then picked up my phone to see if I had missed any calls.

No calls and no texts.

So that meant whoever was currently trying to break down my front door didn't have my phone number.

"It's barely even light out," I grumbled as I reached for a robe and wrapped it around me, dragging my mass of curls into a loose bun on top of my head. Making my way downstairs, I shushed Hank and pulled the door open quickly. In retrospect, I should have peeked out the window first. But I'm never at my best so early in the morning.

The steel barrel of a gun entered my house first, and in moments was pressed directly to the center of my forehead.

I blinked in confusion and tried to wave my hand at Hank to calm his barking down.

"Shut the dog up," Nico ordered.

"Hank, hush," I said, but it did little to calm my furry protector. "Listen, he's not going to stop freaking out while you have a gun to my head. Let's just step inside and calm this down for a second."

I prayed Nico would listen to me. A wild light shone behind his eyes, and I noticed the faint beginnings of a bruise around his left eye.

"Fine, back up slowly, hands up where I can see them," Nico ordered. I nodded, following his instructions exactly. Once the gun was removed from my head, Hank stopped barking, but the hair on the back of his neck still stood up.

"Where is he?" Nico enunciated carefully, but I could read the fear behind his words.

"Who?" I asked carefully, easing a step back.

"Chadwick," Nico bit out.

"I… I don't know. Isn't he with you?" I was honestly confused by the question.

"He's been abducted," Nico said carefully, and I started.

It was an interesting choice of words.

"How can you be certain he was abducted? Maybe he's out partying somewhere," I said, careful to keep my face calm, though my mind was racing.

"There was blood. And screams," Nico said, neither his gun nor his gaze wavering from my face.

"Why in the world would you think I'd have him? He's the last person I'd want to kidnap," I spit out, then bit my tongue.

"Because you were the one who said 'trust nobody.' And then he gets taken. The same day you told him to trust nobody. See? I can connect the dots, lady," Nico said, his muscular body all but vibrating with anger.

"Listen, Nico, come on. I just met the dude yesterday. He came to me and requested my services. I didn't seek him out. I didn't ask to go on the boat... yacht," I corrected quickly. "Hell, I didn't even know who the guy was prior to yesterday."

"So use your psychic powers – " Nico waved the gun in a circle, making me wince – "and tell me what happened."

Shaking my head, I just looked at him helplessly.

"It doesn't work like that, Nico, I swear. Just... can you tell me what happened? And I can try to help?" Anything to get him to stop pointing the gun at me.

Nico studied me for a moment before finally – finally! – dropping the gun down by his side. Which in turn freaked me out even more, because now it was pointed in the general direction of Hank – who quickly began to growl.

"Hey, how about this – I'll make some coffee and let

Hank out so he doesn't bother us. You fill me in and I'll see what I can do to help?" I was trying not to oversell the option, but I really, really wanted to get Hank out in the backyard.

"Yeah, yeah, go ahead. I could use a cuppa, I'll be honest. My head is killing me too."

"Ice pack in the freezer," I pointed to the fridge as I all but dashed to the door to let Hank out for his morning business. Carefully closing and locking the sliding glass door, I turned to find Nico slumped at my counter with an ice pack on his eye and the gun in front of him.

"What happened?"

"We was all sleeping, you know? Like it was late, about four, and the party had died out, everyone stumbling off to their rooms. But you know, I always do a perimeter check because that's the job. I heard something strange as I came through the corridor by the main cabin. Like, I don't know, a thud? A thump? Something, and then someone cursed. No big deal, right? Like maybe someone stubbed their toe on the way to the bathroom."

I nodded for Nico to continue as I poured boiling water over my Chemex drip coffeemaker and the heavenly coffee scent began to fill the room. Brown drops of liquid splashed the bottom of the pour-over as I racked my brain for any clues.

"And then, boom!" Nico slapped his hand so hard on the counter I jumped. "I got hit from behind and when I turned – stunned, of course – I got hit in the face and it was lights out."

"That's awful," I said soothingly. You have to be

careful with the male ego. They don't like talking about getting knocked out – or, frankly, anyone getting the better of them.

"When I came to, there was blood in Chadwick's room and he was nowhere to be found. I searched the whole ship, raised the alarm, ordered everyone off the boat, and still nothing."

"How many people were on the boat?" I asked as I slid him a cup of coffee.

"I don't know, maybe fifty total."

"And somehow that led you to me?" I asked incredulously. "I mean, there are plenty of people you could question there."

"Yeah, my partner's doing that right now. But I had a suspicion, and you know what they say: You've got to follow your gut."

"And your suspicion is?"

Nico downed his coffee, and I winced just thinking about swallowing the entire glass of hot coffee in one gulp. I was certain he was doing it as a display of his toughness. Standing, he slid his hand over the gun and held it up again.

"I suspect you'll be able to use those psychic powers to find our boy. You've got three days. Otherwise… bang," Nico said softly, his finger hovering over the trigger.

"But… but I had nothing to do with this! That's not fair! Chadwick is rich as hell, use your security people to track him down. It's not my problem!" I exclaimed as Nico began to walk through my room, whistling as he went.

"It just became your problem. Three days, Althea."

Just before the door closed behind him, Nico poked his head back in.

"Thanks for the coffee."

Chapter Eleven

"I KNEW THAT MAN WAS CRAZY," Miss Elva said as she picked through a box of donut holes. She'd shown up shortly after my SOS text message to her and Luna, with donuts, coffee, and Rafe in tow.

"I see you still house this devil beast," Rafe said, hovering above the couch and sneering down at where Hank wiggled in excitement. For some reason unbeknownst to any of us, Hank could see Rafe. I'm not going to lie – I found it highly amusing when Hank chased Rafe around the house. Rafe felt differently.

"Yes, Hank still lives with me. That's typically how it works when you have a pet," I said, and Rafe sniffed again.

"In my day, he'd be tossed overboard."

"I'll toss you right back through the veil and to your final resting place if you say something like that again," I threatened. Rafe looked at me in shock.

"Now, Rafe, you know Thea loves her some Hank. That was a mean comment. Plus, can't you see she's had no sleep? Look at that hair and those big bags under her eyes," Miss Elva said, slurping her coffee as they both turned and studied me.

"She's looking rough," Rafe agreed.

I threw my hands in the air. "Listen, I had like an hour of sleep before I had a gun put to my head – excuse me if I'm not a fashionista this morning."

Miss Elva raised an eyebrow at Rafe and mumbled something that sounded dangerously like "That's no excuse."

I pressed my fingers to my pounding temples, and took a deep breath before my inner bitch ratcheted up to a ten.

Miss Elva reached over and patted my knee. "Why don't you go take a shower, honey child, while we wait for Luna. It'll wake you up and soothe you at the same time. Nothing like a good shower to calm the mind a bit."

"Fine, but don't let Rafe be mean to Hank or I swear to the goddess above that'll be the last you'll see of him," I snarled, and Miss Elva shook her head as I walked inside.

"She sure is cranky in the morning, Rafe."

I sighed. I was cranky today, but I would have to say it was justified. You'd think the people in my life would be more understanding when I had a gun waved in my face.

Except that wasn't all that unusual anymore, I realized, as I tossed my robe on the floor of the bathroom and stepped into the now-steaming shower. Ducking my head under the stream of water, I leaned my forehead against the wall and inhaled deeply. The warm water soothed the tension in my neck, and the knot in my stomach loosened slightly.

And wasn't that just what Cash had been saying to me

for weeks now? Somehow over the past year, I'd found myself in numerous life-threatening situations – far more than an average person – and I could certainly understand how it was beginning to wear on him. Hell, it was wearing on me. But it wasn't like I had purposely sought out dramatic situations to throw myself into. It had just been a series of events that had led to other events and before you know it, I'm floating away in the ocean or locked up in a toolshed somewhere.

You know, just another day here in Tequila Key.

I didn't really see any way around it. I mean, I could move, stop reading tarot, make new friends, and live in a gated community somewhere in Naples. And a piece of me would die inside every day I woke up and smiled brightly at Cash and made nice with his country club friends and acquaintances.

And that was no way to live. Even for love.

Damn it, I liked my life here. I liked my friends, where I lived, and I had a thriving business. Aside from a few near-death experiences, I was living my perfect life. So why did I have to be the one to change?

I squeezed my eyes shut to stop the tears that threatened. I had to remind myself that I was a bit in shock and running on little sleep. Plus, I was fairly certain that time of the month was around the corner. All valid reasons to get a little weepy in the shower. But, never one to find self-pity a valuable use of my time, I straightened up and ran my hands through my dripping curls.

I needed to find Pharma Boy, feed Hank, and figure out my love life. Not necessarily in that order, either.

Luna's voice floated up to me as I came downstairs in

a bright blue and white maxi dress, my hair still wrapped in a towel. Stopping by the cabinet that housed Hank's food, I opened the bin, knowing I wouldn't have to even call him to have him come running. Sure enough, as soon as Hank heard the lid of his food bin being lifted he came racing inside, all but tumbling over himself in his excitement. I wish my life was that simple, I thought, smiling down at Hank's sweet face.

"Bon apetit, buddy," I said, scratching his head as he danced around his dish.

"You look better," Miss Elva observed as I stepped back outside. My back porch had a covered area where I'd thrown some pretty couches and had huge plantation fans installed that swoop lazily and distill the humidity in the air on really hot days. Luna was curled up in the corner of one of the couches looking positively casual for her, in faded boyfriend jeans and a brilliantly red top. A funky turquoise necklace hung from her neck and her hair and makeup were perfect. I sighed and sat down.

"I swear you two bitches use magick to look this good in the morning," I grumbled as I reached for my coffee.

Miss Elva slid a look over at Luna. "Told ya she's cranky."

"I'm sure I would be as well, after such a rude awakening," Luna said smoothly, smiling over at me. "Now, tell me everything. Miss Elva gave me the low down on your little yacht party yesterday."

"That's all I know. I didn't even know the dude prior to this and now I'm being held accountable for finding him. It's total BS." I shoved a donut in my mouth to stop myself from wandering into petulant territory.

"Okay, so what we know is that Nico heard a thump, then he got knocked out. So that means there was more than one person," Miss Elva said, pointing her donut at me.

"Ah, good point. Yes, that would indicate two people. Unless the thump was unrelated. But let's assume more than one person," I said. "Then what?"

"Well, if they knocked Chadwick out, unless a guy is really strong, they'd need two people to carry the dead weight. Plus once they get off the boat, they would need a driver, right? Is the marina covered by security cameras? I'm sure the yacht has cameras. I wonder if they could check the footage to see the make of the car."

I picked up my phone and texted Nico the question regarding the security cameras. He'd left me his card with instructions to call when we'd found Chadwick, but since he'd thrown this mess in my lap, I was going to make him do some work too.

"So who wants to kill Chadwick? Or who would profit the most from killing him? Abducting him?" Luna asked as she leaned over and studied the box of donuts carefully.

"Pretty much everyone, that's sure enough," Miss Elva laughed, her emerald caftan fluttering around her.

"It's true. I'm fairly certain everyone on that boat hated him – including his best friend," I agreed.

"Did Victoria?" Luna asked curiously, and Miss Elva and I spoke over each other.

"She's pregnant!" we both said.

"With his baby?" Luna's eyes went wide.

"Yup, and he doesn't know," Miss Elva said.

"Plot twist," Luna muttered. "So if the wife knew – would she come after him?"

"I honestly don't know. Frankly it didn't seem that unusual for Chadwick to be partying with all those girls. I can't think that any woman wouldn't figure it out. I just have to wonder if she didn't care – maybe she was in it for the money?" I honestly couldn't understand anyone marrying Chadwick for love.

"Yeah, maybe they're one of those couples with an open relationship," Miss Elva observed.

"I could never do that," Luna admitted. "I'm way too jealous."

"It's probably easier when you have houses in six different countries and don't see each other all that often," Miss Elva said.

"So where do we start? Can we do a finding spell?" I asked Miss Elva. Between her and Luna, I figured we'd be able to do a few spells, track the billionaire jerkoff down by noon, and I could go back to my very important quandary of whether I should swear off all men for the rest of my life.

My phone dinged with a text.

"It's Nico," I said, reading the text and my eyes going wide.

"What?" Luna asked.

"There was no getaway car. And he's freaking out. Turn on the TV – the news leaked."

Chapter Twelve

"CHADWICK HARRINGTON HAS BEEN ABDUCTED," a chirpy blonde-haired woman read from the teleprompter. I swear she could barely contain her glee at reading the story.

"Wow, so this dude really is the most hated man in America."

"Oh he's up there, that's for sure." Luna pursed her lips as she studied the TV. We listened to the newscast basically tell us everything we already knew.

"A tip has just arrived which suggests that more information will be forthcoming shortly," the announcer paused as she listened to her earpiece. "Apparently… on a website? A website will be set up. Where's Pharma Boy dot com." Her eyes crinkled as she repeated what she was hearing and her lips quirked at the name of the website.

"Pulling it up," Luna called, already at my kitchen counter on my laptop.

Miss Elva and I leaned over Luna's shoulder as we waited for the website – which I'm sure was receiving millions of hits as we spoke – to load. Rafe floated behind us, muttering curses at Hank.

The screen was black for a moment, then a cartoon version of Chadwick's head popped up and began to dance and twirl around the screen as "Ob-la-di, Ob-la-da" by The Beatles played in the background. Clearly, whoever had put this website together had a sense of humor.

Chadwick's cartoon head faded as words appeared on the screen.

"So far this year, Chadwick Harrington has not only patented and received approval for an Alzheimer's cure, but has also privatized the sale of that cure and insisted on making it available only to the wealthiest of people," I read as the words scrolled past. "This is wrong."

"It is wrong," Luna said softly behind me.

"Because Chadwick has never had to bear the humiliation, suffering, and sorrow that comes from loving someone with Alzheimer's or being diagnosed with the disease, it's necessary that Chadwick learn humility. Stay tuned as we all watch Chadwick's lesson on this week's episode of As His World Burns."

"Holy shit," Miss Elva breathed.

"He's turning it into a soap opera," I murmured.

"The whole nation is going to tune into this," Luna said.

"The FBI will trace the website's IP address pretty quickly," I said, crossing my arms across my chest as I thought about this. "We don't even need to bother to look. It'll be shut down ASAP." I couldn't help but feel relief at being let off the hook.

"I doubt it. I don't think someone would have gone to

this level of planning and left themselves easy to locate," Luna said.

"Criminals aren't always smart," I retorted.

"My first instinct is that it's someone with a family member who has Alzheimer's," Miss Elva said, meeting my eyes. "Can we get some records or at least full names of his inner circle?"

"On it." I texted the request to Nico. His response, which his saintly Catholic mother would certainly not approve of, was not very polite and I told him as much. Finally, he agreed to get us some information.

"I mean, what does he expect? We just blindly use our psychic powers to find this jerkoff?" I said, walking to Hank's toy drawer and pulling out a stuffed carrot. Hank danced around me until I tossed it across the room, then went tearing after it.

"I say we do a drive-through of Tequila Key. Go check out the boat. See if we pick up any vibes. If nothing else, it'll be something to start with until we get more concrete information or until this website drops more clues."

"Fair enough. Let's roll."

Chapter Thirteen

"YOU KNOW WHO you should be calling now, don't you?" Miss Elva said over her shoulder. We'd all piled into Luna's car and I was monitoring the situation on my smartphone.

"No, who?" I asked, barely glancing up from the news report I was scanning.

"Really, Thea?" Luna asked.

"What?" My brain was clicking pretty slowly this morning.

"Cash? You know? The cyber-security whiz?" Miss Elva said, and Rafe snorted next to me. I shot him a glare before taking a deep breath and looking up at the roof of the car for a moment.

"I can't call Cash. This is the kind of stuff he hates. He walked away from me because of these types of situations. The last thing he wants to deal with is me explaining that I have to find some over-entitled jerk or I'll be sleeping with the fishes in three days."

As if on cue, my phone buzzed with an incoming call. I grimaced as I read the display.

"Which one of you witches did this?" I hissed.

"Not us, child, not us." Miss Elva promised, though I saw a small grin hover on her lips. Apparently my love triangle was providing great amusement for her.

"Hey," I said softly into the phone, staring out the window as the houses of Tequila Key passed by.

"Tell me you aren't involved in Chadwick's abduction," Cash said immediately, bypassing any pleasantries.

"I can very much assure you I did not abduct Chadwick," I said heatedly.

"That wasn't what I was asking," Cash pointed out and I pressed my lips together. I'd hoped he wouldn't notice that I hadn't directly answered his question.

"Um, define involved," I finally squeaked out. I saw Miss Elva shaking her head.

"Damn it, Althea. This is a big deal. How could you get yourself involved in this?" Cash was all but shouting.

"Hey! That's not fair," I shouted right back. "I didn't ask to be involved in this. I was brought into it. Now I have to find him in three days or I'm… in big trouble."

Dead silence met my ear for so long that I began to worry he'd hung up on me.

"I told myself I wouldn't do this," Cash finally said. "I told myself I would walk away from you. That I would be done with you and the messes you keep getting pulled into. That I would date other people and settle down and everything would be fine."

I blinked against the sudden press of tears in my eyes.

"And?" I whispered.

"And I can't stop thinking about you. It drives me mad. I shouldn't be so involved, I shouldn't be risking myself and my reputation to help you out of situation after situation," Cash ranted. I let him continue. "And yet, I'm drawn to you. I can't seem to stop thinking about you. I can't seem to stop calling. I can't stop worrying about you."

"So what are you saying exactly?" I asked, closing my eyes as a swirl of hope hit my stomach.

"I don't know. I don't know what the answer is. You don't want to live my life and there's no point in asking you to. It'd be like putting a hibiscus in a closet without sun. You'd wither and die. I don't want to change who you are."

"But?"

"But I don't know if I can live with the stress of constantly worrying about your safety either," Cash sighed, knowing that he was just circling around himself.

"So where does that leave us?" I asked softly, my eyes trained on the line where the ocean met the sky. They lived harmoniously, I thought. Never meeting, never interfering with each other's essence. Why couldn't Cash and I be like the ocean and the sky?

"I have no idea," Cash admitted. "Part of me wishes that I'd never met you."

Ouch.

"Awesome," I said, closing my eyes again, my emotions in turmoil as I leaned my head back against the seat rest.

"And part of me can't imagine living without you."

I straightened up at that.

"Really?"

"Really. So, there's that. Here I am pouring my thoughts and feelings out to you at eight in the morning because I'm terrified you'll be in danger again. And you say nothing," Cash groused.

"Well, I'm in the car with Luna and Miss Elva," I said quickly, wanting him to understand why I wasn't exactly outlining all my feelings to him at the moment.

"Ah. I see," Cash said, and silence met me again. Cash and I both knew I would tell Luna and Miss Elva everything we said anyway.

"Listen, I don't know what to think or feel. I'm not sure I could live with knowing that your family would feel like I was a constant disappointment, you know?" I admitted finally, digging my nails into my palms. "And I love being with you when it's just us, but I'm not sure I'm the right person to stand by your side for corporate functions and stuff," I said, looking down at the tattoos that covered my arms.

"What if I don't care?" Cash shot back.

"You should, though. You should care about what impressions you make with clients. It's your business," I pointed out.

"And my personal life has nothing to do with my business. Jesus, Althea, it's not like you're a felon or something."

Well, I had been taken into custody a time or two, but no need to bring that up at the moment.

"I think we need to talk more about this," I said, not sure where this conversation could go for now. "However, I guess I could use a little help if you have a moment to spare."

"Finally. Only took you an entire novel to get there," Rafe grumbled next to me, and I raised my hand and made the sign of the cross at him. He cowered back into his corner, and I kept him pinned there with my glare.

"What do you need?" Cash's sigh was audible through the phone and I pictured him running his hand through his thick dark hair.

"Well, since we do need to find Pharma Boy, I'm wondering if you could maybe run some security stuff and see if we can track the website?"

"Althea, the best minds in the government will be doing this. What makes you think I can do better?"

"Um, because you're brilliant?"

Flattery will get you everywhere, ladies.

"I don't know about that. But I'll see what I can do. Anything else?" Cash asked.

"I mean, we need to see if we can get into the security footage. Oh, and he was taken away on a boat. So he has to be somewhere that isn't all that far, I guess. Like maybe we could zero in on the WIFI point? Signal? Something?" I trailed off, realizing just how little I knew about technology and how things worked.

"Oh, is that all? Just track a boat in the middle of the ocean by tapping into satellites and radar. Hey, why not see if there are any submarines out there and get some sonar going too?" Cash asked, his tone light and breezy. I knew he was annoyed.

"Never mind, I guess it's stupid."

"I've got a big deal going through in the next couple of days. However, I'll do what I can," Cash said. "In the meantime, can you do something for me?"

"Sure, what?" I asked, twirling a purple curl around my finger.

"Don't be stupid. Don't put yourself in stupid situations. Assume the worst of everyone. And stay in touch with me, even if it's just text messages. The press and a gazillion other people are about to descend like locusts on Tequila Key. It's going to get crazy. Take care of yourself."

I hadn't thought about that.

"Promise," I said, and we said our goodbyes and hung up. Neither of us said "I love you." I don't think either of us knew where we stood on that front anyway.

"Cash said the press is going to descend on the city. It's going to be a shit-storm," I said, putting my phone in my lap.

"Gee, you think?" Luna asked, gesturing through the front window. I gasped.

The main street of Tequila Key was bumper-to-bumper traffic, which was unheard of in our little town. News vans had quite literally stopped in the middle of the street, and reporters lined the sidewalks while cameramen dodged the locals and tried for the best shot.

"It's madness," I breathed.

"And it's only going to get worse," Miss Elva warned.

Chapter Fourteen

"BOY, WERE YOU RIGHT," I said to Miss Elva as I scanned my phone. We'd pulled a U-turn and taken a side street to wander our way toward the yacht and away from the reporters. The yacht was surrounded with police, FBI, and news vans.

"How come the FBI is involved?"

"Probably got called in for a high profile case," I murmured, watching as Chief Thomas gestured angrily to a Fed.

"Poor Chief Thomas. This hit fast and furious," Luna said and we all hunkered down to watch.

"It's too hard for me to get any reading with all this energy in the air," Miss Elva admitted, and Luna and I both agreed.

"Way too much distraction. Maybe we need to approach from the water?" I finally asked, knowing that meant I would need to tap Trace for use of his dive boat.

"Call Trace?" Luna asked immediately.

"I suppose," I shrugged, wondering how I felt about that after having just gotten off the phone with Cash.

"What's with that face?" Miss Elva said, and I realized she was staring at me over her shoulder.

"I don't know. It seems like I'm always relying on men." That wasn't really what I was prissy about, but I didn't have the emotional wherewithal to deal with examining my feelings for either of these men at the moment.

"Child, please. You ain't relying on no man. You're just using the tools at your disposal," Miss Elva chuckled and Rafe bristled next to me.

"So I'm just a tool?" Rafe snarled and crossed his arms to look out the window.

"I'd say you're a tool," I murmured and Rafe went into a fit, whipping himself into a tizzy next to me.

"I will not be talked to like this by some… tarot card reader," Rafe sneered at me, "Know your place, woman, or I'll have ye walk the plank!"

I snorted. I couldn't help it. Sure, Rafe used to be a pirate, but that was several hundred years ago. He needed to get up to speed on how things worked now.

"Well, Rafe, see, you can't make me do anything. Not only because Luna and I will send your ass home, but also because women have equal rights in this day and age," I said, smiling sweetly.

"Kind of," Luna murmured.

"Kind of. It's better than it was, at least," I admitted. I wasn't about to go into wage differences and reproductive rights with a pirate ghost.

"From where I sit, seems like all you do is moon after

men anyway. I suspect we still have the control," Rafe shot back and I raised an eyebrow as I saw Miss Elva straighten up in the front seat. Biting my lips, I waited.

"Rafe, I know you aren't implying that these beautiful, intelligent, and highly powerful women spend all their time moping after men. Because if you were implying that, you'd also be saying that the only thing on my mind is chasing men and I think we both know that isn't true. However, I'm more than happy to stop trying to solve this here situation and go chase after men. Many men," Miss Elva threatened and Rafe trembled in mid-air.

"But, but, my lovemountain! You're a goddess. Nothing and no one is more stunning than you. I bow to you and your immense beauty. Please don't look for other men. I'm your man. I will love you eternally," Rafe rambled, desperation in his eyes.

"Now who is mooning after whom?" I murmured and Luna snorted.

"My lovemountain is different!" Rafe snapped at me. "She's nothing like these basic men you run after. She's extraordinary."

"Though I can't argue with me being extraordinary," Miss Elva chuckled, "you need to stop, Rafe. Men and women chase after each other equally in this day and age. Women don't wait around for men to take care of them anymore. They can run their own lives and businesses while still finding an equal partner. It's just how it is."

"Yeah, Rafe, so shut it." I stuck my tongue out at him.

"Real mature, Thea," Luna said.

"I'm not feeling mature. I'm tired and cranky. I don't

want to have to find some dipshit that I'd rather was dead anyway. He deserves everything coming to him," I said.

"Is that so?"

My stomach flipped as I turned to find Chief Thomas standing next to the open window of the car.

"Um, maybe?" I squeaked.

Chapter Fifteen

"HI, CHIEF THOMAS," Miss Elva said, and Luna and I nodded our hellos. I actually liked Chief Thomas, and he had been helpful in saving our lives in the past. Not that I needed to get into all that at the moment.

"Why am I not surprised to see you ladies out here?" Chief Thomas said, pushing his sunglasses up on his nose as he leaned down to look in the car. I was grateful that he couldn't see Rafe as, at the moment, Rafe was making faces at the police officer.

"Just checking things out," I said, smiling brightly up at him. "You know, all the gossip and all."

"Uh-huh. And what makes you think you need to locate Mr. Harrington?" Chief Thomas said, not believing a word I said.

"Did I say that?" I wondered out loud to Luna, who rolled her eyes at me. "I don't think I said that."

"She definitely didn't say that," Luna agreed.

"I'm pretty sure that's what I heard. But I don't have time to deal with you three right now." Chief Thomas looked over his shoulder to the FBI agent who was calling to him. "Just… don't do anything stupid. And at least keep me in the loop on anything you find. That's all I'm asking."

It was a fair request – since we were technically withholding information on an investigation – and I nodded my assent. As Luna pulled the car away from the melee, she glanced back at me.

"Seems like everyone's always telling us not to do anything stupid."

"I know. It's getting really annoying," I said. I was picking up my phone to text Trace when I caught the alert on the newest development in the Chadwick case.

"Ho. Lee. Shit."

"What!" Miss Elva turned all the way around.

I held my phone up so she could see the image of a naked Chadwick, dressed only in a diaper with a sucker in his mouth, that was pasted across the front page of WheresPharmaBoy.com.

"No!" Miss Elva squealed and grabbed my phone. Luna immediately pulled the car over to the side of the road and we all leaned in to look at my phone.

"Living with Alzheimer's can be embarrassing to both the person afflicted and the family members who can end up being caretakers. Since Chadwick Harrington doesn't understand embarrassment, we are delighted to present you with the first in one of many embarrassing reveals we'll provide this week. Stay tuned for the next episode of As His World Burns," Luna read.

All three of us took a collective inhale before we squealed, laughing as we looked at the picture. I'm not saying it was very adult of us, but, hey – we all have our moments.

"Is it immature of us to laugh over this?" I asked.

"Yes," Rafe sniffed from the corner and I shot a glance at him.

"Why, Rafe? Does this hit too close to home?" We all squealed in laughter again and Rafe just shook his head at us.

"You ladies shouldn't be making fun of a man just because he likes to dress up a certain way."

"Why? Men pick on women all the time. Change your hair color, get a boob job, wear heels, put on makeup. The least we can do is have a little fun," Luna complained.

"What's a boob job?" Rafe asked, his interest piqued at the mention of nudity.

We all stilled at that. How do you explain inserting silicone parts into the human body to a four-hundred-plus-year-old pirate?

"It's a medical procedure. To enhance a woman's bust line," Miss Elva finally said, and Rafe crowed in delight.

"You should do that," Rafe said, nodding at Luna, who looked at the ceiling of the car, clearly counting to ten in her head before responding.

"There's a lot of things I should do. Like banish you forever. It's just a ways down my list," Luna said sweetly, and Rafe went back to cowering in his corner.

"Perez Hilton picked it up," I said, looking at my phone and laughing as I read the famous gay blogger's delighted takedown of Chadwick's, er, lack of goods.

"He suggests that Chadwick is overcompensating for his dinghy with the size of his yacht," I laughed. I couldn't help it. I knew it was mean and that the guy was probably begging for his life somewhere – but hey, he hadn't exactly endeared himself to me. Or anyone else, really.

"I like that," Miss Elva decided as we pulled away from the media circus. "I'm going to ask you that after your next date – if you took a ride on the dinghy or not."

"Mathias has a yacht, thankyouverymuch," Luna murmured and we all smiled at that. Luna's boyfriend, a doctor and all around hunk, deserved to be well-endowed.

"Althea?" Miss Elva asked and I raised an eyebrow.

"Do you see me dating anyone?"

"I see you dating everyone," Rafe said, a look of contempt on his face. Oh, yeah, like I needed to be slut-shamed by a pirate, of all things.

"I can date anyone I please, Rafe. It's really none of your business and I certainly don't appreciate your judgment," I said stiffly, crossing my arms over my chest.

"I told you she was cranky today," Miss Elva warned Rafe.

I just shook my head, picking up my phone to text Trace. He got back to me immediately.

"He'd already planned on cruising out and checking things out. Boat leaves in twenty."

"Perfect, just enough time to grab snacks," Miss Elva said.

Snacks. At a time like this? I could only shake my head. But I'd be lying if I said I wasn't craving a few munchies myself.

"Fine, we'll have an early lunch on the boat. Let's stop at the market for sandwich fixings."

Chapter Sixteen

"NOW THAT'S JUST COLD-BLOODED," Trace whistled when I showed him the picture of Chadwick on the website. The ensuing media response had been predictably sensational, with #babydinghy now trending on Twitter and Facebook. The picture had apparently launched a vitally important debate on Fox News about whether a man could dress like a baby in the bedroom, and things had gone downhill from there.

Or uphill, if you took delight in reading those kinds of stories. I'm not saying I don't take a peek or two at gossip blogs once in a while… okay, fine, I have a subscription to *US Magazine* and read my stories every week. Don't judge. How else am I supposed to know which Real Housewife got in a fight at the Four Seasons or which celebrity was canoodling other celebrities? It's very taxing keeping up with it all.

"What's cold-blooded is Chadwick withholding a cure for Alzheimer's," I reminded Trace as I hopped back on the dock and unwound the rope while he reversed the boat.

We worked together so seamlessly on the boat that I didn't even have to think about it.

"You're right, he's an awful human being. Still. If that's what the website is leading with – I can only imagine what the rest of the reveals will be."

"Well, whoever's running this site is smart to lead with something sensational. I just hate when I get all excited for a new show and then they lose me after the first episode, you know?" Miss Elva asked.

"Yes, they need a strong hook to keep you coming back," Luna agreed.

"So whoever's running the website came out of the gate swinging."

"And he hit it out the park, that's for sure," Miss Elva said as we motored down the channel and out toward open water. I took a deep breath; the water immediately soothed me.

"So what are we looking for here, ladies? I was just going to check out all the press madness from the water. I'm interested to see what you think you'd find just by looking at the boat."

"Unless you look in the water under the boat," Miss Elva said and I craned my neck to look at Trace. It hadn't occurred to me to dive around the yacht. I wondered if the FBI would have divers in the water or if they would take the webmaster's word for it and assume that Chadwick was being held alive.

"We could get wet," Trace said, winking at me to make his double entendre clear. Like I needed help figuring that one out.

"Maybe not right now? When there are police, FBI,

and hundreds of press around? They'd probably see the boat and our bubbles."

"Sure, give it a day or two to die down. They won't hang out on the boat all the time."

"In the meantime, we wanted to get a feel. Use our witchy senses and see if we can pick up on any vibes," Miss Elva said easily. Trace, completely used to our weirdness, didn't even blink.

One point in the Trace column, I thought.

Not that I was thinking about Trace. Or his tanned muscles, since he wasn't wearing a shirt today – a decision I'm certain he made on purpose so I would drool over his eight pack and tattoos. Nope, I wasn't noticing a thing.

Trace motored the boat toward where the yacht was moored. It seemed we weren't the only ones who had thought to check out the scene from the water. A gleaming white and red coast guard boat patrolled the area directly around the yacht. A man in uniform stood at the bow and shouted something through a bullhorn at a smaller boat of what looked like men with cameras.

"Press," Luna said.

"I'm not surprised. They'll do anything to get a good shot," Miss Elva said, "That's how they make the big bucks. Selling photos to those trashy magazines."

Both Luna and Miss Elva turned to look at me.

"What? Don't act like you don't read them too," I said, pointing a finger at Luna. I'd seen her steal my magazines more than once.

"Oh, we all do. Let's not pretend we don't," Luna grumbled as Trace guided the boat away from where the yacht teemed with activity.

"Huh," Trace said, glancing down at his computer.

"What?"

"Nothing, just – for a moment there, all my instruments were wiped clean. And my compass went into a tailspin."

"Really?" I wandered over and looked past the steering wheel to see the display up and running.

"It's fine now. But it blinked out. For just a second there. The compass thing throws me even more," Trace said, glancing over his shoulder and at the yacht. Pulling out a tiny stub of a pencil, he checked the coordinates and noted it in his logbook.

"Think it's something important?" Luna asked, stretching her arms over her head.

"I think I've learned that when investigating anything with you gals, I pay attention."

Trace had a point. It was best not to ignore anything that could be a clue.

"Let's think about it then. What would cause a compass to go screwy? And what would wipe the computers? And why?"

"Magnets," Miss Elva said immediately.

"What?" I shaded my eyes with my hand and leaned forward to look at her. "Why magnets?"

"Isn't that the whole Bermuda Triangle superstition? That it's a magnetic field that wipes out all the instruments and compasses? It's also why mystics are drawn to the area. Vortexes and whatnot." Miss Elva shrugged, her eyes still scanning the yacht. "He's definitely gone."

"Who's gone?" I had trouble keeping up with Miss Elva sometimes.

"Chadwick. His energy signature is gone from the yacht. Nico's up there. And there are a lot of bad people on the boat."

"What do you mean by bad?" Luna asked, squinting at the yacht.

"Just the same as I felt yesterday. Chadwick had very few actual friends. Most of the people who hung around him did so for the money."

"That's his own fault. He could've been a decent human being and made real friends," Luna pointed out.

"Some people are never taught how to be decent human beings," Miss Elva reminded her. "We don't know what led to him being what he is. But right now we have to figure out how to find him. As much as I'd like to wash my hands of this mess and let him suffer – it's not what decent people do."

"Plus Althea's ass is on the line," Luna added.

"Pssh, her ass is always on the line." Miss Elva shrugged.

"Gee, thanks, guys."

Chapter Seventeen

TEQUILA KEY WAS OVERRUN, to say the least. I elbowed my way through a line of people to the bar where a very harried Beau was working with his new bartender. Lucky's was packed wall to wall with people and a line snaked out the door. The only other time I'd seen it like this was for a New Year's Eve party one year, with an under-the-sea theme.

"Seats, there," Beau barked and pointed to three seats with reserved signs in front of them. Smiling at an annoyed group of women who hovered behind them, I slid onto a stool and held the others out for Luna and Miss Elva. Trace had declined to join us, saying he had a whole slew of customer emails to respond to.

"Now back off, ladies. No need to be pressing up on me. You'll get served when you get served. Pissing me off isn't going to make it go any faster," Miss Elva said, and the women shrank back. I bit back a grin. I loved Miss Elva's complete lack of a filter.

Beau slid a mojito in front of me, a Corona in front of

Miss Elva, and a vodka soda with lime in front of Luna without asking us for our order.

"Food?" Beau asked and we all shook our heads no. He nodded once and disappeared with a promise to talk when he could. I didn't blame him – while this was good for business, it also came at a difficult time for Beau, what with him trying to open his new place on schedule.

"Is Beau still dating Cash's brother?" Luna asked.

"I have no idea." I really didn't. But it still bothered me that Cash's family had no problem accepting a gay relationship into their fold, yet a tattooed tarot reader was shunned. So much for being all-inclusive.

"So what's next, ladies? We need an action plan," Miss Elva decided.

"Well, Trace and I will dive at some point when things calm down. But I think we need to widen our water search. Also, I'd like to find out if any of Chadwick's friends or co-workers have a family member who suffers from Alzheimer's. I asked Cash and Nico to get me that info. This strikes me as really personal. So the only place I can think of starting is there," I said, sipping my minty drink and trying to drown out the surrounding chatter that was suddenly reaching a higher pitch. "What is going on?"

"A new reveal on As His World Burns," Beau said, rushing past us with three drinks in his hands.

"What! Already?" I pulled my phone out and scanned the website, Miss Elva and Luna's heads close over my shoulders.

"Mistress Number Four," I read, my eyebrows rising at a black and white photo of Red Bikini from yesterday. It read like a mugshot, with a full picture of her facing the camera and her details listed along the side in typewriter font. "Mistress Number Four is Tara Palwa, age twenty-four. Occupation: whore; favorite hobbies: whoring, breaking up marriages, having anxiety attacks, and being decidedly unintelligent. Little known fact: Miss Palwa is Chadwick Harrington's fourth, and least-liked, mistress. She is outranked by several more who precede her in many levels of affection, which Chadwick doles out as he sees fit. Note: All mistresses are aware of his wife. Wife is unaware of mistresses."

"Well, she's aware now," Miss Elva said, shaking her head at my phone.

"Where is the wife? What does she look like?" I wondered. So far we'd delved into Chadwick's personal business, and that read lover to me. I suspected his wife had to be behind this. I mean, would a business rival be getting all personal right off the bat?

I googled for images of Chadwick's wife and a brunette – pretty, albeit in a clean outdoorsy way – popped onto the screen.

"Connecticut," Luna said immediately, and I had to agree. She looked like she had just stepped out of a Ralph Lauren catalog – complete with a cable knit sweater and a yellow lab. All she needed was a steaming cup of coffee in her hand as she sat by a firepit at their cedar shake Hamptons home.

"I wonder if she's old money, too. She looks it, in that sort of 'I'm casually rich and don't have to show it off' kind of way," I said. Miss Elva hummed her agreement next to me.

"Completely different than the mistresses too," I

pointed out. "So, Chadwick doesn't have a type, necessarily."

"Has the wife been interviewed?" Luna asked and I scrolled through the news reports.

"So far all we have is a 'No comment' from the wife, it looks like," and then I looked up when the crowd noise rose again. "Again?"

"Pull up the site," Luna said, raising a finger at Beau for another round of drinks. It looked like we were about to get another installment of As His World Burns.

Another drink later and we were definitely feeling the buzz of excitement in the room – and maybe a bit from our drinks. The website had graciously revealed two more of Chadwick's mistresses, one of whom I recognized as one of the women who had been sunning themselves by the pool yesterday. I wondered if either woman had known about each other.

I wondered if Victoria would be revealed.

"Speaking of mistresses," I said, sliding a glance at Miss Elva, "did we figure out if anyone on the boat is missing? Like, is Victoria accounted for? Nathaniel? Shannon?"

"Ah, we did not do that." Miss Elva nodded at me.

I texted Nico – *Is anyone missing from the boat other than Chadwick?* – and waited. This time he responded quickly, saying that everyone was accounted for and being questioned by the FBI.

Anyone being held as a suspect?

No. Everyone is being released but being told to stay close.

"Interesting," I said and read the texts to the girls. So

the FBI wasn't pointing any fingers yet. I wondered what 'keep close' meant. Not leave the town? The state?

"I wonder if they'll reveal Victoria? If so, would that eliminate her as a suspect?" Luna asked, taking a delicate sip of her vodka soda.

"Or would that be the perfect thing to do? Expose her secret in order to hide her involvement?" Miss Elva asked.

"Both good questions," I agreed, then realized that my eyelids were beginning to droop closed. "Ladies, I have to go lie down. Between one hour of sleep and two afternoon drinks, I'm about to fall asleep. Let's reconvene later."

"Perfect. I'll go jump Mathias," Luna said, then blushed. I realized she hadn't meant to say that out loud.

"Sure, rub it in," I grumbled as we waved goodbye to Beau, knowing he would put our drinks on our monthly tab. He nodded at us and the crowd immediately swallowed our empty chairs. In moments, we'd pushed ourselves outside and past the long line.

"You bitch!" I stopped in my tracks when I heard the squeal.

The entire line of people turned to see Tara Palwa, in a screaming pink Disney t-shirt and mini-skirt, launch herself at the other woman I had recognized from yesterday. We all gasped as they both went down on the sidewalk, rolling and screaming at each other as hair was pulled and faces were scratched.

"Shouldn't we break them up?" Luna said, looking back at me and then giving me a disapproving look when she saw that I was recording the fight on my phone.

"What? This is good stuff right here," I said, refusing to apologize. I winced as Tara got a good hair tug in.

Mistress No. 3 was not to be outdone, though, and promptly flipped Tara over and sat on her.

"He's mine!" Tara wailed, trying to squirm her way out from under the leggy brunette.

"You're fourth – didn't you see that? You're nothing. Just a whore. And I let you borrow my Balenciaga bag, too. You owe me big time!" the brunette shouted, then squealed when Tara pinched her.

"You don't even care about him! You just want his money!" Tara screeched, trying unsuccessfully to roll away from the brunette.

"*Everybody* wants his money! You can't pretend like you're in it for love!" The brunette screeched right back, then twisted Tara's arm behind her back and shoved her face into the ground. As pins go, it was very successful.

"After seeing the picture of the little man downstairs today, I don't think anyone is in it for the loving," Miss Elva said, and half the line who had heard her broke out in laughter.

"And yet he still managed to get all these women hooked on him," I murmured, watching as Tara once again tried to pull herself from under the brunette. Finally, I heard yelling and saw a deputy I didn't know race over and lift the brunette off Tara.

"That was worth every bit of the last two days," I decided, hitting save and immediately uploading the video to Facebook.

What? I don't know anyone who wouldn't do the same.

Chapter Eighteen

"HEY! MY VIDEO IS VIRAL!" I exclaimed as Luna drove us home.

"Mhmm, child, and so am I. Look," Miss Elva held the phone up to show me that WheresPharmaBoy.Com had stolen my video and posted it as the next installment of As His World Burns. Beneath it, the hashtag #ILoveMissElva was trending, and it appeared you could purchase Miss Elva trucker caps directly from the site.

"How? I can't… it's been like five minutes!" I said, completely amazed at the quick work behind this website.

"They've clearly got a good team working on this," Miss Elva said, and I saw her click a button on the phone.

"Did you just purchase a Miss Elva hat?"

"Obviously," Miss Elva said. "I can rock a trucker hat, right?"

Luna chuckled. "You can rock anything, Miss Elva. You make everything look cool."

"I'm going to get a couple colors, I think." Miss Elva

bit her lip and scanned the options as I shook my head from the backseat.

"You want one?" Miss Elva asked and I rolled my eyes.

"Fine, I'll take hot pink if they have it," I grumbled, annoyed at myself for wanting one.

"They have a black one with hot pink writing."

"Fine, great, get it," I said, all but racing from the car in my need to get to a bed. Any bed. Just to close my eyes for a moment and not talk to anyone anymore. I was clearly getting delirious if I was buying Miss Elva trucker hats.

"What are you doing here?" I gasped as I pushed the door open to find Cash unpacking take-out on my counter. I'd forgotten I had given him a key.

Cash turned and seared me with his gaze. My insides went liquid as I studied him, trying to keep my anger with him at the forefront of my mind when all I wanted to do was devour him like the donuts I'd had for breakfast this morning.

"I took the company helicopter down. I figured if I was close, at least I could try to keep an eye on you."

I swear, if I was a dog, my hackles would have risen.

"I'm capable of minding myself, thank you very much," I said, crouching down to pet a vibrating Hank, who carried the carrot toy in his mouth. I tugged it gently from his mouth and tossed it across the room without looking.

Cash leaned against the counter and crossed lightly tanned arms across his blue pinstripe button-down shirt. He was a man who filled out a suit well, and I was a woman who cringed at the thought of pearls and panty-hose. Where could this relationship go?

"I'm well aware that you're a functioning adult. Is it so hard for you to accept that someone cares about you and wants to help?"

I straightened and met his eyes.

"I suggest you lead with that next time. 'Hi, Althea. I came down because I care about you and want to help you.' Not insinuating that you're here to look after me like I'm some wayward child with no capability for managing my life or making good decisions." My nose couldn't have gone any higher in the air if I had tried.

"This from the woman who has somehow had her life on the line at least three or four times since I've met her?" Cash raised an eyebrow at me.

"Purely by chance," I sniffed and crossed to the counter, stopping a foot away from Cash.

"Yet the common denominator is you," Cash said softly, his handsome face wreathed in concern.

"Listen, if you flew all the way down here to lecture me, you can just go ahead and hop on your kajillion-dollar helicopter and fly right back. I'm exhausted, I'm sick of people telling me what to do, and I have zero patience for this control routine you're trying to pull on me. So unless you plan to make nice and be quiet, I suggest you leave." I glared at him to let him know I was serious about him leaving – and I was… up until he pulled me hard against his chest.

I kept my arms crossed and resisted for a moment, until I realized just how comforting his arms were. And just how much I wanted a hug. I sniffed a little as I burrowed my face into his chest, inhaling his delicious male scent – a blend of soap and spice – and relaxed marginally as his arms pulled me tighter.

"You can't even hug me?" Cash whispered into my hair and I sighed, unhooking my arms and wrapping them around his waist, pressing my body to his as we swayed slightly, just absorbing each other's nearness.

"Why is it so hard with you?" Cash murmured.

"I don't try to make it hard. It just is. This is my life. This is who I am, who my friends are, and sometimes that means we get into weird situations. I won't apologize for it. I will say I'm sorry if I worry you or scare you. It's not my intention. I certainly don't enjoy having my life threatened either," I spoke into his chest, my words vibrating back against me from his comforting warmth.

"I don't know if I can ever stop worrying about you," Cash said and I pulled back to search his face.

"But can you accept me for who I am? All the weirdness and abnormal non-corporate stuff? Will you accept that?"

Cash paused, his grey eyes searching mine, before he answered.

"I'm trying."

It was an honest answer, and one that I deserved. A part of me wished it had been an unequivocal 'yes.' But in that instance, I probably wouldn't have believed it. The fact was, I appreciated his honesty more than anything.

"Then that's all I can ask for," I said.

Cash reached up and ran a hand over my curls, tugging a particularly purple one from the bunch.

"Nice hair," he said, his lips quirking in a sexy smile.

"Thanks. I was in a mood."

"I like this mood," Cash said, his lips coming down to brush mine softly. "Does it extend to what you're wearing beneath this dress?"

"I'm not wearing much under this dress," I admitted, my body heating to his touch.

"Even better."

Chapter Nineteen

I CAN'T SAY there was much sleeping done during what was supposed to be my nap time, but I felt revved up and energized as I lay next to Cash and ran through the sequence of events so he could get up to speed.

"I still don't understand why this Nico guy is forcing you to find Chadwick? Can't you just tell Chief Thomas that he's threatening you and have him put in jail?"

Huh. That hadn't occurred to me.

"Well, because it's my word against his. I have no evidence," I said, feeling a bit dumb.

"Weren't you texting him?"

I thought about the text messages we'd been sending back and forth, but doubted there was anything incriminating in them. If anything, their focus was on what everyone in Tequila Key was trying to figure out – who abducted Chadwick Harrington?

"Probably nothing useful. Listen, the chief has enough on his hands. It's a madhouse down here. The sooner we can help make some headway in this case, the sooner we can resume life as normal."

"It's too bad your normal and my normal are so different," Cash said and I stilled, pulling myself away from where I'd been cradled in the crook of his arm.

"Yes. Isn't it just?" I said. He called my name but I ignored him as I went into the bathroom and turned the shower on. Annoyance lanced through me as I thought about how this topic would be a constant refrain. Maybe we really were just too different.

"I'm sorry," Cash said from behind me and I jumped, ducking my head under the showerhead and then cursing because I hadn't wanted to wash my hair. Resigned, I let the stream pour over my head as I closed my eyes for a moment.

"You can't have it both ways," I finally said, refusing to turn around. "You can't have me be what you want me to be and still love me. Because if I change for you then I won't be the woman you claim to care about anyway."

I sighed as Cash stepped in the shower and wrapped his arms around my waist, pulling me back against his chest.

"I don't know how to come to terms with not wanting you to be in harm's way, while also accepting your lifestyle."

"You either have to work on it, accept it, or walk away," I said, my eyes still closed against the stream of water that buffeted my face.

"I tried walking away," Cash said, his voice a warm timbre against my ear.

"Then it seems we're at an impasse," I said.

"I can accept who you are and what you do – I admire it. But you're going to have to give me something – some way to try and keep you safe. Otherwise I'm going to go crazy if we continue this relationship."

And there it was – the big "if."

I thought about it. In this moment – cocooned in his arms, with the steam of the shower wafting around us – I wanted to be with him. But I couldn't ignore my feelings for Trace either. And just what kind of person did that make me? Not that Trace was bringing much to the table, as far as actually trying to date me. I mean, Cash had brought me take-out, for God's sake.

Was that all it took to woo me? Some paper cartons of Japanese food?

"Well?" Cash said and I snapped back to the present.

Oh, right. Cash wanted an answer on how I could make his life less stressful.

"Perhaps I can text you more often?"

"Can I put that trace program on your phone again?"

Just the thought annoyed me – knowing that my whereabouts would be monitored at all times.

"I mean, that's not my favorite idea," I admitted, reaching for the coffee mint soap Luna had made for me.

"It's not like I'd be tracking your every move. I do have a life and a thriving business, as you know," Cash said, taking the soap from my hand and beginning to scrub my back. I moaned a little as he swept soothing circles over me.

"So what would be the point then?"

"If I haven't heard from you in a while or if I get an SOS from Luna, I could track you easily."

"And if I don't have my phone?"

"Then I'll send out the dogs."

I laughed and leaned back against him. I supposed every relationship needed some give and take.

"If you promise to be cool with what I do for a living and if you stand up to your family, I might be willing to let you track my phone," I said.

"Gee, thanks, dear," Cash said and I laughed again, turning to wrap my arms around his neck and kiss him.

"I guess I'm not quite ready to give up on this. But I'm also not that good at doing all the right 'girlfriend' things in a relationship either," I admitted against his lips. The water was beginning to cool, but my libido was certainly not.

"Why don't we just try and figure it out together then," Cash said against my lips and swallowed my reply with his kiss.

You wouldn't hear any arguments from me.

Chapter Twenty

AS I ATE cold Japanese noodles from the carton, I half-listened to Cash handling a business call on his phone. He looked relaxed now, wearing loose linen pants with his legs kicked up on my couch, and his muscles well-defined in a black t-shirt. I found my eyes tracing the line of his muscles through the t-shirt and my mind getting distracted from the task at hand. My phone vibrated in my lap and I pulled my eyes away from the delicious man on my couch.

Are you awake? If so, turn on the TV.

It was Miss Elva.

I texted back confirmation as I turned the TV on low. It was still on the same news channel from this morning, though this time the news announcer was a cheerful brown-haired man with blindingly white teeth. A clip of a man clad in a grey business suit being led away in hand-cuffs was highlighted with the words: *Pharma Boy's CFO arrested on allegations of insider trading.*

"Well, well, well," I murmured, keeping my voice low

as Cash was still talking. Picking up my phone, I pulled up As His World Burns to read the latest installment.

CFO Stanley Worchester and Chadwick Harrington knowingly engaged in insider trading when purchasing controlling stock of competitor, Well General. Phone records and emails detailed below.

I scanned the records, my eyebrows hitting my hairline. Naughty, naughty, Pharma Boy, I thought and walked out to the porch to call Miss Elva.

"Damn, he's in big trouble," I said without preamble, immediately bending over to toss a stick for the wagging Hank below me.

"Sho is, child, he sho is," Miss Elva echoed back.

"So the Feds are for sure staking their claim on this case now," I said, tugging the stick from Hank's mouth and throwing it again. I could throw for him for hours and he wouldn't tire.

"Big time. But I'm wondering – if they find insider trading, what happens to shares of Well General? And if they were one of his biggest competitors, would that mean they had also had a way to manufacture this Alzheimer's drug?" I asked.

"Or if they had a better way of processing the formulation, they could get around the patent," Miss Elva mused and I raised my eyebrows. I was glad she wasn't there to see me. To this day, Miss Elva still surprised me with the depth of her knowledge on a wide range of topics. Most people dismissed her as a crazy backwater witch doctor – but they had no idea that beneath the flamboyant caftans and big earrings lay a brilliant mind.

"I honestly don't know how that works," I admitted,

"but I can have Cash research it. Do you think this is the ultimate goal here? Not just to punish Chadwick for being a jerk, but to release the patent somehow?"

"I'd have to assume that's the larger goal. Or, I suppose, I can only hope. Too many damn people suffering out there," Miss Elva said. I heard her speak away from the phone for a moment. "Rafe wants to know if you've bedded Cash again."

I rolled my eyes.

"Tell Rafe it's none of his damn business."

Miss Elva relayed the message and then chuckled.

"Now, Rafe, you know Althea can get any man she wants. Enough of your nonsense."

"I swear to God…" I threatened and Miss Elva chuckled again.

"Child, he just likes getting a rise out of you. Don't let him bother you much. He's harmless."

"Yes, his ability to decimate an entire Valentine's Day party is quite harmless," I grumbled, shoving my hand through my hair, then pausing when I realized Cash was standing in the door.

"I'll call you later. Keep me posted on any leads," I said hastily and ended the call.

"Ah, the infamous Valentine's Day party," Cash said, his face beginning to look thunderous. We'd never really discussed what had happened at the party.

"I'm sorry, Cash. I am. I obviously wouldn't have done anything if we had been together," I said, my hands fluttering lamely in the air.

Cash's forehead creased as he sat on the chair next to

me and automatically reached down to tug the stick from Hank's mouth.

"And you say you were drugged..." Cash said, raising an eyebrow at me.

"Potioned," I corrected him, knowing how ridiculous it sounded.

"Right, a love potion. And this potion bends free will?"

"Um, not so much that as it makes people less inhibited. More willing to act on any feelings of attraction," I said and then clamped my lips shut. Goddess help me, I was not going to tell him the potion was only supposed to enhance feelings that were already there.

But he found his own way to that conclusion quickly.

"So you're attracted to Trace," Cash said, crossing his arms over his chest and staring me down.

"I mean, yes, but not like I'm attracted to you – it's just..." I sighed and seriously considered tugging my hair out. "Yes, I do find him to be attractive. That doesn't mean I think we would work as a couple, okay?"

"But you haven't tried. How would you know?" Cash said, his voice low.

"I'm not sure I want to try. I like our friendship as it is. I don't want to lose it," I admitted, tugging at a loose thread on the cushion beneath me.

Cash sighed and scrubbed his hands over his face.

"I'm putting it on record that I'm not exactly happy about you hanging out with him. But since you and I are still figuring things out – I can't forbid you. Tell him that I may have to hunt him down if he makes a move on you again, though."

I bristled at that, but since he was technically being

pretty fair about the whole situation, I, for once, listened to my better half.

"I'll relay the message."

The doorbell rang, distracting me from the conversation as Hank went into a fit of barking and raced across the room. This time I peeked out the window before opening the door. See? I can learn lessons. A UPS van was pulling away from the house and I tilted my head, wondering what I had ordered online that I had forgotten about.

Picking up the small box, I nudged the door closed and pulled at the tape holding the folds closed.

"Shut up," I said, pulling out a black trucker hat with 'I love Miss Elva' written on it in hot pink. Instead of the word 'love,' a bright pink heart was emblazoned in its place. A piece of paper fluttered to the floor and I bent to pick it up, marveling at the print and delivery speed of whomever was manufacturing these things. Hadn't Miss Elva just ordered these a few hours ago?

"What's that?" Cash said from the door. I put the hat on, tilting my head to pose for him.

"Shut up. She has a hat line now?" Cash's mouth quirked in a smile.

I filled him in on the details as I unfolded the piece of paper.

"Shit," I said as I read the note.

"What?"

"If you really love Miss Elva, you'll find Chadwick… or prepare to never see her again," I read out loud, my palms trembling. I almost crumpled the note up before Cash snagged it from me.

"Nico," we said at the same time, and I grimaced.

Chapter Twenty-One

"IT DOESN'T EVEN MAKE SENSE," Luna said, pacing my living room. "We're already looking for Pharma Boy. Why the threat?"

"I don't understand what Nico's trying to pull – or maybe he's simply coming unhinged," I said, running my hands through my curls. Cash massaged my shoulders, which helped a bit with easing my tension. I felt restless, though, like I needed to be doing something. Just sitting here and talking about what-ifs would get us nowhere.

"You'd think that with the new interest from the FBI, they would be locating Chadwick quickly. Why go so far as to abduct Miss Elva?" Cash said, his hands working magic on the knot in my shoulder.

"That's the wife," Luna said, and I turned to see a news clip of the wife being hurried into the police station downtown, throwing her hand up to block her eyes from the thousands of flashes from the news stations' cameras. She wore a loose linen sheath with a chunky gold chain link necklace that screamed money.

"She seems fairly put together for someone whose husband has just been kidnapped," I pointed out, noticing her makeup wasn't smudged and her hair had the look of a fresh blowout.

"Can you read her?" Luna asked quietly, freezing the TV screen so I could see her face more clearly.

"Let me see. It's never quite the same as me being with someone in person, but I can try," I said, stepping closer to the TV to examine her face and see if I could get any sort of extra-sensory insight. I stared at her eyes, trying to pick up on a flash of emotion or anything from her.

"She's annoyed. More than anything. She's annoyed that she's been thrust into the spotlight and she's pissed off that she has to deal with this."

"But she's not worried about him, is she?" Luna said, crossing her arms and studying the frozen image on the screen.

"Nope. Which just moved her to the top of my suspect list," I said.

"Why?" Cash asked, his surprise genuine.

"Because if she's not even remotely worried about him, maybe she's in on it? I have to wonder if anyone in her family suffers from Alzheimer's. Can you run that somehow?" I directed that question at Cash.

"But if dude is as bad a husband as it seems, perhaps this is just one more thing she has to deal with," Cash said, grabbing his laptop to begin a search. "I mean, come on, would you be happy if some website was showing all these awful things your husband has done or is doing? I'd probably be fed up and annoyed too."

The man had a point. I'd be far more than annoyed, that's for certain.

"I don't know… I just feel like she's involved in this somehow. But I don't have enough to go on," I admitted.

We all jumped as my front door blew open, a shocked Hank going into a cacophony of barking as he raced across the room.

"Miss Elva!" I gasped, delighted to see her unharmed, pushing a tied-up Nico in front of her. The man's head hung low and he refused to meet our eyes. I couldn't tell if he was more embarrassed that Miss Elva had gotten the better of him, or ashamed of taking her to begin with.

"I see y'all are terribly worried about me," Miss Elva huffed as she pushed Nico further into the room.

"We were very worried. That's why we got together. To meet and discuss a strategy for how to find you," I pointed out, watching as Rafe hovered quietly behind Miss Elva, his expression grim. "What's up with Rafe?" I asked, forgetting that Cash couldn't see the pirate ghost.

"He got a little shook up when Nico here decided to get physical with me and there wasn't much he could do to stop him," Miss Elva said, pointing to a seat. Nico sank into it, his arms tied behind him.

"How come he's not talking?" I asked, studying Nico a little more closely.

"A spell," Miss Elva said simply.

I walked over to wrap my arms around her. "I'm glad you weren't hurt," I whispered.

"Child, it takes more than some muscle from Brooklyn to take me down," Miss Elva said and I smiled against her shoulder before releasing her.

"How'd you get away?"

"Did you get hurt?"

"How'd he abduct you?"

"Was he the one running the hat orders?"

Luna and I peppered Miss Elva with questions until she put her hands on her hips and glared at us both.

"Why don't I just tell you what happened?"

"Yeah, that'd be great. Beer?" I asked, already moving to the fridge and pulling out a Corona. I knew Miss Elva's preferences.

Miss Elva settled herself on a bar stool at my counter and I slid her a beer while Luna and I stood in the kitchen. Rafe floated behind Miss Elva, for once ignoring Hank.

"So, this fool comes and jumps me in broad daylight as I'm about to climb my porch," Miss Elva said without preamble, taking a swig of her beer and shaking her head at Nico's foolishness. "I decided I'd go along. I didn't need him shooting any paint chips off my new shutters. Plus, he had the gun at my temple all dramatic-like. Again, let me remind you, in broad daylight."

"Wow, he's getting sloppy."

"I wonder what's in it for him to find Chadwick? Is he that concerned about losing his job?" I asked, moving to the liquor cabinet to pull out a bottle of vodka. I held it up in question to Luna and she nodded.

"So this idiot holds a gun to my head and ushers me into the van. I get tossed unceremoniously inside, and you know how I feel about my green caftan. But he doesn't bind my wrists and he also doesn't take my bag away."

We all shook our heads at that. Everyone knows Miss Elva's bag of tricks is bottomless.

"I decided I'd just lean back and relax and see where he would take me. Maybe I'd pick up some clues."

"While I was in hysterics," Rafe sniffed and Miss Elva turned to smile at him.

"You did just fine, sweetie." Turning back, Miss Elva raised an eyebrow at us. "Rafe decided to punch the horn on the van, which caused this fool to lose his damn mind until he pulled over. I never did get a chance to see where he was taking me because he turned the gun on me. I suppose he figured I was doing some sort of witchcraft – you remember how crazy he was about the whole reading when we came to the boat," Miss Elva said to me.

"So he's screaming at me to stop with the horn, Rafe's having himself a fine ol' hissyfit and trying to choke him, which is making Nico lose his shit because suddenly he's struggling to breathe."

"I almost got him," Rafe said proudly and Miss Elva laughed.

"You sho did, honey, you sho did." Miss Elva beamed at Rafe. "At that point, I saw Nico was about to tip over into crazy-land; his gun hand was shaking and he was choking. So I essentially just put a freeze spell on him."

"A freeze spell?"

"It's almost like giving someone a lobotomy. It just wipes everything for a moment, and then I take control." Miss Elva shrugged.

"Like hypnosis?"

"Kind of, but without leading someone into it by verbal commands. Also, you know, without their will," Miss Elva shrugged again. No big deal.

My mind was reeling with the possibilities of such a spell and its potential uses.

"Would that mean we could question him?" Luna asked and I nodded appreciatively at her. Smart woman.

"Go right ahead, child. He's just chilling."

Luna and I moved to where Nico sat, lounging in my red leather chair and staring mindlessly across the room. Hank sniffed his feet curiously and then went back to following Rafe around the room, his head cocked inquisitively.

"Hey there, Nico, how's it going?" I asked softly, not wanting to startle him. I wasn't sure if I could knock him out of the spell.

His eyes met mine and I could see that a spark seemed to be missing behind them. It was as though the lights were on but nobody was home.

"Hi Althea," Nico said.

He remembered who I was, so that was a step in the right direction. Miss Elva hadn't wiped any thoughts or memories – she'd just taken over his free will.

"Why do you want to find Chadwick so badly?" I asked.

"I need this job."

"Yeah, but can't you find a security job anywhere? You're obviously a dedicated employee," I said soothingly.

"I get paid more at this one."

"How much more?"

"Side deals," Nico murmured, and I raised an eyebrow at Luna.

"Side deals how?"

"Part of my job is to look and see everything. Some of

the things I see… I get paid extra to pretend I never saw. And I need the money."

Luna and I paused at that and I suspected we were both thinking the same thing – just how much did we want to know about what Nico had seen in Chadwick's employ?

"I'd be careful there," Cash said, coming to stand by me, "If you discover something that pertains to a crime you'll have to tell Chief Thomas, and then you won't be able to explain just how you found it out."

"Yeah, but we can always make something up to cover ourselves," I pointed out. I gave Cash a little frown and decided upon, "Why do you need the money?"

"Gambling debts," Nico said immediately and I sighed, the tension loosening my shoulders a bit.

"Ah, I see. You owe money. And all these bonuses that Chadwick gives you go to paying your debts."

"I suspect he also uses the bonuses to gamble more," Luna whispered, but Nico heard her and nodded, his eyes sad.

"I can't seem to stay away. I always think… just one more hand. And that'll be my ticket out. I can take my Ma to the beach and set her up in a little house somewhere."

Sighing, I scrubbed my hands over my face. My read on Nico had been correct from the beginning. I kind of liked him and knew him to be good at his job. Learning of his gambling addiction only made me feel a bit sad for him.

I decided to change tactics.

"Who do you know who would want to embarrass him like this? Does anyone who works for him have family members with Alzheimer's?"

"I think everyone wants to see him embarrassed," Nico said, his eyes staring off across the room again. "He's not a nice person. He does whatever he wants, whenever he wants. And it doesn't matter who he hurts along the way. His wife, his friends, his girlfriends… everyone has a reason. I've been going over and over this and it's almost like there are too many strings to pull."

"And you thought forcing the psychics to help would cut down on your work," Luna said, letting her tone go a little harsh.

Nico shrugged, unapologetic. "Pretty much. I mean, it can't hurt, right? You all can use your magick to cut down on the amount of information that I have to wade through."

"Sorry, buddy, it doesn't quite work like that," I said, annoyed with Nico and the fact that he didn't realize some of his boss's traits had rubbed off on him – namely, being entirely selfish in the pursuit of his own wants and needs.

"What do we want to do here?" I asked, turning to look at Luna and Miss Elva. "Can you make it so he doesn't bother us anymore?"

"I can put the suggestion in his brain that he is only here to help us – not cause harm," Miss Elva shrugged, "but I can't promise anything. I can only control his free will for so long."

I heard Cash mutter under his breath behind me and I shot him a glare.

"Let him go. And suggest he leaves us alone. I don't want the pressure of finding Chadwick on our backs anymore," I finally decided.

Miss Elva nodded, telling Nico to get up and follow her outside.

"Well, that's that, then, right? No need to find Chadwick and you can let the police do their work, right?" Cash said brightly from behind me.

I turned to him, surprise lancing through me. "Don't you know us at all?" I asked. I mean, I know he'd met me and been involved in more than one situation with me. Did he honestly think that Luna and I weren't going to try and figure out what was going on with Pharma Boy?

"After all this? You'll still try to find him?" Cash's face flushed and I saw him work through a range of emotions.

Luna looked between us.

"Should I go?"

"No, you stay. You obviously have criminals to run down since, you know, you're highly trained in doing that," Cash said, sarcasm dripping from his voice. He stood up and closed his laptop. "But that's fine. You just keep doing what you do. Put yourself in danger. Run magick spells. Talk to stupid pirate ghosts. Oh, and speaking of, hey, Rafe. Thanks for drugging Althea so she messed around with Trace. Super awesome of you." He was all but shouting by the time he finished and I bit my tongue, not wanting to mention that Rafe had followed Miss Elva out.

Luna crossed the room and slid out the backdoor, taking Hank with her into the backyard.

"I swear it feels like we just had this conversation, oh, I don't know –" I pretended to check my watch – "like a few hours ago?"

"Yeah, well. Talking about it and the reality of it can be a bit different. Here I thought you had actually listened and were going to try not to make stupid choices. And then there's spells and kidnappers and ghosts, and you still involving yourself in dangerous situations when your involvement is unnecessary. I just… I don't even know anymore. I swear I'm going crazy. You make me crazy."

Heat pumped through my blood – and not the good sexy kind. The kind where I felt like the anger started in the pit of my stomach and spiraled its way up through me until I felt like my head was going to explode.

"Well, maybe you make me crazy. Did you ever think about that? You swoop down here, all good-looking and rolling in money, and sweep me off my feet. Then you get mad when I'm not what you want me to be? How is that remotely fair to me? I was doing just fine before you came along – now here I am wondering do I have a boyfriend, do I not have a boyfriend? Will his snobby rich family disapprove of me? Should I try to change my life for him or just continue being me? Frankly, none of this is fun," I said, finding myself dangerously close to tears.

"Maybe we need to adjust our expectations of each other," Cash finally said.

"Or maybe it's too soon to have any expectations. Did you ever think of that? Maybe we just need to throttle way back. And, you know, date without expectations."

Cash tilted his head, his grey eyes narrowing.

"Like… casually? Just sex?"

"I don't know. But maybe we're trying to shove this relationship into a box that it just isn't going to fit into." I had finally admitted the truth we had been dancing around for a while. Maybe our two different worlds just couldn't fit together. Or maybe we wanted different things in life.

And just how did physical chemistry and mutual compatibility play into traditional relationship expectations?

"I care about you, Althea, a lot," Cash said, crossing to wrap his arms around me.

"I care about you, too," I said, leaning into his warmth for a moment.

"But maybe we need to care about each other from afar. Or perhaps with different expectations?"

"Play it loose? Date when we feel like it? Date other people?" I asked, my voice tripping a bit over those words. I wasn't sure what that would look like; I could only imagine how distracted I would get thinking about Cash dating other women. And wasn't that just the pot calling the kettle black, I thought as my mind wandered over to that night on the boat with Trace.

"An open relationship without it being an open relationship? Like… I'll see you when I see you?" Cash said, trying to keep his voice light.

"I guess just that we admit we have a connection with zero expectations," I finally said, feeling like my heart would crack, yet knowing that this was probably the best choice for us. At least until he could fully accept my life.

And a part of me doubted that he ever really could.

Chapter Twenty-Two

"CHILD, YOU KNOW restricting yourself to one man is just foolish," Miss Elva said as we settled into our seats at Lucky's an hour later. Luna had come back in from outside, taken one look at my face, and gone into triage mode.

"I don't know. I don't seem to mind it," Luna said, examining the chip bowl in front of us before systematically picking the perfect fried tortilla chip.

"Thanks," I said, cramming three chips into my mouth.

"I'm sorry, that was rude," Luna said, reaching out to squeeze my arm. "I just meant if you find someone who totally accepts you for who you are, is all. Then it's nice to be with just one person. But you can also go by Miss Elva's philosophy and wear caftans, travel the world, and leave a string of lovers in your wake."

The idea was beginning to hold some appeal.

"You know, I was motoring along just fine before Cash came into my life," I said, taking a sip of my mojito and glaring over the rim of my glass. "I was happy."

Luna and Miss Elva both went silent, studying their drinks carefully.

"What? I was," I protested.

"Child, you were doing just fine. But you seem happier when you're dating someone, is all. You know, regular bedroom sessions will do that for a woman," Miss Elva said.

"Yeah, yeah, I'm aware," I grumbled, just now realizing it was going to be a long time before my next bedroom session.

A harassed looking Beau rushed in the door, pushing through the crowd to slip behind the bar.

"Ladies. Shit is hitting the proverbial fan," Beau said without preamble, and we all gaped at him.

"What's up?"

"Did you see the latest installment of As His World Burns?" Beau's voice went up in pitch at the end of his question.

We all grabbed for our phones, and I noticed the rest of the bar was collectively inhaling.

"Oh no," I breathed.

A single black and white image dominated the front page of the website, and I cringed at the words beneath.

Bouncing bundle of joy expected in six months. To mistress #1! Please congratulate Victoria on their love child.

I cringed as I read the words, wondering just how this would impact things.

"I can't help but feel bad that this got revealed," I admitted, pushing my phone away glumly. I noticed the rest of the diners were gossiping and laughing about it. I suppose that's what soap operas were – just one more big dramatic reveal. They were removed from it all and just watching it unfold. But I actually knew Victoria – and though I didn't like her, I did feel bad for her child.

"The wife is losing her shit all over the main street as we speak," Beau said, leaning in. "Like having a full-on temper tantrum about the news. I can't say that I blame her."

"Does anyone know where Victoria is?" I wondered.

We all shook our heads and Beau just shrugged. The last I had seen Victoria, she was talking with the FBI by the yacht. I sincerely hoped she had a security detail in place, or she was about to get mobbed.

Beau leaned over the bar and snagged my hand. We'd had very little best-friend time of late, and though I didn't blame him – what with opening his new restaurant and the shit-show that was currently Tequila Key with the nation watching – I did miss him.

"What's up with you? You don't look so hot," Beau said.

I shrugged one shoulder. "Cash and I broke up. We just can't seem to come to terms with accepting each other's lifestyles."

Beau's handsome face creased in sympathy for a moment, and he patted my hand. "You never know unless you try. Don't let this close you off from dating. We all take chances with our hearts when we meet people. I'm just sorry this didn't work out for you. Because I think Cash is an intrinsically good guy. I think he's just too caught up in the trappings of societal expectations."

"You'd think with all his money he'd feel comfortable living outside those expectations," Miss Elva chimed in.

I nodded at her. "Right? Isn't that the point of making all that money? To give you more freedom in how to live your life?"

"Some people need the expectations of society to guide them," Luna pointed out, and I sighed, feeling imminently grateful that those same guidelines didn't bind me.

"If it makes you feel any better, I haven't heard much from that cute brother of his either," Beau said, and I realized what a bad friend I'd been by forgetting to ask Beau about his own relationship.

"I'm sorry – I can't believe I haven't asked you about that," I said, taking a sip of my mojito and sighing.

"It's fine. I've barely been around. And we didn't get too far along the dating path anyway," Beau said, grabbing a towel to dry glasses and studiously ignoring the line of customers waiting for his attention. "Though he was handsome as all get-out, I kind of felt like I was just his fun plaything, not someone he was going to take seriously."

"Like they're just slumming with the likes of us?" I muttered, annoyed at myself for even saying the words.

"You knock that shit right off," Miss Elva said, throwing me a stern glance. "Money doesn't make for anyone being better than anyone else. You are two of the finest people I know. If anything, you both were slumming by dating those two squares."

I gulped past a giggle that threatened to explode as Beau's face creased with his blindingly bright smile.

"As always, Miss Elva, you are the voice of reason.

Forget those men… we are amazing and don't need them coming down here and critiquing our lives. Onward and upward!" Beau said, tapping his glass to mine and I silently echoed his cheers.

Onward and upward, indeed.

Chapter Twenty-Three

I WAS one mojito past my typical drink limit, but I didn't care all that much. I had no readings in the morning and had essentially just been told that my lifestyle made me non-dateable.

Therefore, a slight buzz was allowed.

Luna had dropped me off and after making sure that there were no tears imminent, had retreated to probably curl up with her delicious and lifestyle-accepting boyfriend. Not that I was bitter. I loved Luna and wanted her to be happy.

"At least I have you, right, Hank?" I patted Hank on his head where he'd curled up by my side in bed. It was a bit early for me to go to sleep, but after the days I'd had of late, I didn't care. Sometimes nothing fixes things like pulling the covers over your head and tuning the world out.

Unfortunately for me, tuning the world out seemed to be something I was not going to be allowed, as my phone buzzed with an incoming message.

"They just found Victoria's body. Call you shortly."

I sat up and shoved the covers back, my heart pounding as I thought about what this could mean. Had she been murdered? It was one thing for Pharma Boy to be abducted, but going after Victoria seemed unnecessary. I gripped the phone and waited on Miss Elva to call me.

"Honey child, she done took her own life," Miss Elva said as soon as I answered her call. My heart sank and I closed my eyes as sadness washed through me. Such a senseless and unnecessary loss of life, due to one person's vendetta against Pharma Boy.

"And her baby's life," I whispered, angry at her selfishness. Her baby had never even been given a chance.

"This is real bad, child, real bad. Now the FBI is doubling down even more. Who's to say what will be revealed next and who it could harm? This started out shocking and funny, but it's just taken a real bad turn," Miss Elva said.

"What should we do? Think we should try going out on the boat? I'm not sure what that will even do, but maybe we'll pick up on something." I scrubbed my eyes with my fists as my head pounded dully with sadness and a sense of helplessness that I wasn't used to feeling. Typically, with my extrasensory abilities, I had a leg up in difficult situations. But Victoria's suicide had blindsided me.

"We might as well try going out on the boat. Nothing else can be done about it," Miss Elva said.

"I'll call Trace. Let's go at dawn."

Chapter Twenty-Four

IT WAS A quiet group that motored out on the boat as the sun creased the sky. Luna huddled with a cup of coffee and a loose sweatshirt while Miss Elva sat up front and stared out at the water. It seemed no one was in the mood for conversation this morning.

Trace leaned against the captain's chair, a red windbreaker tossed over his shoulders, and his blond hair pulled into its typical nub at the base of his neck. Glasses shaded his eyes against the light of the rising sun, but I swear I could feel his gaze burn through me when he turned and looked at me.

"So you broke up with Cash?" Trace said without preamble, and his lips pulled up at the corners in a bit of a smirk.

"How did you know that?" I asked, glaring up front at where Miss Elva studiously ignored us. It looked like someone was meddling once again.

"Word gets around. Small town and all." Trace shrugged.

"Yes, we broke up. Happy?" I don't know why I was being cranky to Trace; it wasn't really his fault we had broken up. I guess I didn't like seeing the satisfaction on his face.

"Yup, I absolutely am," Trace said, his teeth flashing white in his tanned face as he grinned at me. I couldn't help but feel my own smile threaten to break out. Damn him for always making me want to laugh.

"Great, I'm glad my heartbreak makes you happy," I grumbled.

Trace moved so suddenly, I barely had time to register that he was in front of me and studying my face carefully, his sunglasses now shoved up onto his head. "Are you really heartbroken?" he asked carefully, his eyes boring into mine.

I shrugged a shoulder and looked away from his relentless gaze for a moment before looking back up.

"I'm sad, but I'm not heartbroken. I wasn't in love with him."

There, I'd said it out loud. And maybe, just maybe, admitting that would take the sting out of Cash's rejection.

"Good. That guy didn't deserve you anyway," Trace said, running his thumb lightly over my bottom lip and sending a shiver through my very core. I mean, I'm human, okay? My body certainly remembered the steamy night we'd had on the boat on Valentine's Day, even if my mind had tried to push it away.

"Is that so? And you do?" It seemed I was trying sassy on for size this morning.

"Nobody deserves you, but I hope I'm lucky enough to have you someday," Trace said, his eyes still holding mine.

I gulped. See? This is why I should have just kept my mouth shut and not tried on my sassypants. It never went well for me.

"Then you best be asking her out on a real date, and none of this expecting to shack up without putting any effort in. Althea deserves someone who will woo her," Miss Elva chimed in from the front of the boat.

Oh sure, *now* she wanted to talk.

"Well, Althea? What do you say? Will you let me woo you?" Trace said, crossing his arms over his chest as he studied me.

I swallowed as my blood seemed to heat from within. There was no denying my attraction to Trace; it was more that I was concerned about my heart with him – and the potential for losing one of my best friends.

It seemed we'd already jumped past the point of no return the night of the Valentine's Day party. Either I had to take a chance on this or let the question of 'what if' always simmer below the surface of our friendship.

"Yes, I'll let you take me on a date," I said, amending his words because I couldn't quite bring myself to say the word "woo" without snorting. It seemed like such an old-fashioned concept, considering Trace and I had already been one short step away from doing the bedroom boogie-woogie on the front of his dive boat.

"Excellent. Prepare to be wooed, my woman," Trace said and snuck in a quick kiss before turning back to the wheel, whistling a jaunty tune.

I was glad at least one of us was in a good mood because now my stomach was turning over in knots. "I wouldn't say I'm your woman," I said, crossing my arms and glaring at him. He was acting like this deal was already sealed.

"Yet," Trace said, shooting a cocky grin at me. I caught myself trying not to laugh once again. Damn that man.

I moved to where Luna sat at the back of the boat and sat next to her, needing a moment away from Trace to focus on what we were actually doing out here this morning. Luna silently offered me her to-go cup of coffee and I took a sip, appreciating the hazelnut creamer she had added.

"Picking anything up?" I asked, my eyes scanning the land as we motored from the channel and out toward sea.

"Kind of hard to pick anything up, what with all those lust vibes floating around between you and Trace," Luna said, but there was no sting in her voice as she bumped my shoulder with her own.

"Yeah, I wasn't expecting that today," I admitted.

"It's fine. In fact, it's more than fine. I suspect this will be good for you both. Time to grow up and try out a real relationship with someone you actually respect."

"Wait, what's that supposed to mean? I respected Cash." Hadn't I? I mean, I'd thought we'd been doing a pretty good job of dating as adults.

"I don't think Cash was ever a real threat to you. At least not to your heart. Trace, though? Yeah, you've already shown you guys can be best friends. So when you sign up to ride this ride, just remember that this could actually be the real deal."

Well, shit.

"I'm not sure what that would even look like, to be totally honest," I said, stealing another sip of her coffee.

"Maybe you need to just let it unfold and not put any expectations on it? Or not try to control it and shove it in some sort of box or make assumptions?" Luna said.

"Easy for you to say," I grumbled. But I knew she was right. Perhaps the best thing I could do for myself and my heart was to just live in the now.

"It's always easier on the outside looking in. But just know that I love you and I'll always be in your corner – no matter what kind of crappy decisions you make," Luna said with a wink and I bumped her shoulder again.

"Careful or I'll toss you off the back of this boat," I said and she laughed.

"Althea – check out those boats," Miss Elva called from the front and I straightened to see where she pointed to a row of yachts anchored off the shore. Yachts were only allowed to anchor in designated areas so as not to damage the reefs. Tequila Key had seen an influx of boats, given the national news focused on our tiny little town and the drama that was currently unfolding.

I studied the line of boats, but aside from the fact that they screamed money to me, I wasn't entirely sure what she was asking.

"What are you getting?" I finally asked.

"There's something there. With the one on the far right? I think there's a vibe. Someone on that boat knows something."

I narrowed my eyes as Trace steered the boat closer. The yacht on the right gleamed in the light of the morning sun, and I saw a crew member mopping a deck. Otherwise, all was quiet on the boat.

"Marigold's Madness," I read the name of the boat and

closed my eyes, focusing in on the name and what it could mean. As I sifted through my impressions, my eyes popped open.

"You're right, Miss Elva. Someone on this yacht is connected to what's going on. I didn't catch it at first, but now I've got it loud and clear."

"You're sure?" Trace asked. I nodded, pausing for a moment to appreciate the fact that he didn't even hesitate to question my psychic abilities.

"I'm not sure what or who, though. But I think we need to do some digging on the owner of the yacht. And who is Marigold? The name is tripping something for me too," I admitted.

"I wonder if the word 'madness' refers to Alzheimer's," Luna said softly and my eyes widened.

"That's an excellent point," I said and I relayed the same to Miss Elva.

"Let's go back. There's not much else we can do here. And it's clear that security doesn't want us moving in too close," Trace said, nodding toward a man who had appeared on the deck, his arms crossed over his chest and a gun visible at his waist.

"Yeesh, they aren't playing around," I mumbled. Just to be an ass, I waved saucily at the man and blew him a kiss.

He inclined his head at me and then disappeared.

"Whoops," I said.

"Sassypants indeed," Miss Elva chuckled from the front.

Chapter Twenty-Five

WHEN I GOT HOME I realized I couldn't call Cash to research who owned Marigold's Madness. Damn it, that was one convenient avenue of cyber security research that I could no longer tap into.

I paused to pull a toy out for Hank and opened the door to toss it into the backyard, an ecstatic Hank chasing after it. I wanted one more cup of coffee before I went into the shop for the day. Heating some up from the pot I had made hastily earlier that morning, I poured a cup and wandered to the couch on my outdoor patio, my mind churning with thoughts.

It'd been a hectic couple days – irrespective of the Pharma Boy situation. How was I supposed to feel about Cash walking out and Trace walking in? It was like my love life had a revolving door and I had no idea who would come through it next.

And wasn't that just my problem? Shouldn't I be the one allowing who and what I wanted into my life?

Mulling over the spark I'd felt for Trace on the boat that morning, I closed my eyes for a moment and tried to actually envision Trace as my boyfriend. What would that look like exactly?

I started as Hank dropped his soggy toy on my lap. Laughing, I tossed it again and returned to my thoughts. I liked my life, I loved my friends, my work, this house of mine and my happy little dog who was currently racing in circles around the yard. Trace fit into it all. He knew me well, understood and accepted what I did for a living and who I was as a person. So what was I so scared of?

Being vulnerable was tough for someone like me. My whole life I'd always put up barriers to protect myself from getting hurt or being made fun of by other kids. It wasn't until I'd met Luna and kind of fallen into my tribe that I'd become more comfortable with who I was as a person and as a woman. Dating had been a trial, travesty, and overall soap opera for much of my life. It wasn't until recently that I'd really even considered seriously dating someone. And that's when Cash had shown up – and Trace had made his feelings known. Funny how life worked, I thought, as I tossed the toy for Hank again. There never seemed to be a right time for anything. Which meant I should just jump in feet first and see whether I would sink or swim.

Lord, I hoped I could swim with Trace. Just the thought of losing him as a friend freaked me out more than I wanted to admit. And yet… Yet there was more that maybe I did need to test out.

My phone beeped. And then rang, and vibrated, and

beeped again, and the doorbell rang. Hank lost it, racing across the yard to bark ferociously at the front door. I closed my eyes for a moment before taking a breath and standing up. I didn't even want to answer my phone – terrified what the news on the other end would be. I was still reeling from the news about Victoria, and I wasn't quite sure what else I could deal with today.

Having learned from dealing with Nico earlier this week, I peeked out my window to see Miss Elva, trucker hat on, turning to yell at a crowd of press.

I cracked the door and hissed "Get in here" at Miss Elva. She slowly walked backward while addressing the thousands of flashbulbs that all but blinded me.

Is it bad that my first thought was to wonder if I had put makeup on this morning?

"Now, y'all are just going to have to back up off this private property now, or I'll be calling the law," Miss Elva intoned, her hand on her hip, her attitude at a ten. "But I'm happy to answer any questions in just a few quick minutes. I'll be needing to consult with my client first. Cheers, loves." Miss Elva tipped her trucker hat, blew a kiss to the crowd, and sashayed inside.

"Child, you sure got yourself in a whole lot of hot water now," Miss Elva chuckled. I just stared at her with my mouth open.

"What in the ever-loving hell is going on?" I hissed as I closed the blinds on my front windows.

"Didn't you see? You're the feature on As His World Burns today," Miss Elva laughed again.

I just shook my head at her. "You cannot possibly think this is a good thing," I said, moving across the room to silence the ringer on my phone. I ignored all the messages and scrolled to the internet, pulling up the website.

"Shit, shit, shit," I swore. The website featured a prominent picture of me, and not the nice glossy professional one from my business website, but one where I was strolling along the street in a maxi dress, my hair wild, and a definite sheen of sweat on my face.

Psychic Althea Rose was one of the last people to see Chadwick Harrington. Her reading predicted he would be in great danger, yet he didn't heed her warning. Can she really see the future?

"You've got to be kidding me," I groaned. I'd been thrown to the wolves. I looked at my phone to see Luna calling.

"Yes, I saw it," I said immediately and Luna sighed. I put her on speaker so Miss Elva could hear her.

"I had to lock the shop. Did you see your online calendar? I think you're booked out for the next six months already and this just hit the website ten minutes ago."

"Really?" Now that was interesting. I mean, I'm not going to say I was unhappy about being booked out.

"Any publicity is good publicity," Miss Elva nodded sagely and I rolled my eyes at her. What was she, my publicist all of a sudden?

"Close the scheduler," I asked Luna. "I don't want to deal with that much of a client-load that far out."

"I already did. I figured you'd be annoyed by being that booked up. Though you are probably the only one who'd ever actually feel that way," Luna muttered.

"Hey, I like some flexibility in my life, okay?" Six

months of booked out clients was already making me feel itchy, and I'd just learned of it less than a minute ago.

"I doubt you'll be getting much flexibility until this is resolved. I just saw a news clip that everyone who is anyone wants to interview you. Hmmm, maybe you could be on *Good Morning America*!" Luna said, her voice cracking in excitement and I groaned again.

"I don't want to be on TV. It adds ten pounds. Probably twenty in my case," I said, feeling decidedly grumpy about the prospect.

"Whatcha trying to say about full-figured women?" Miss Elva asked, hand on her hip and head cocked as she studied me with a raised eyebrow. The trucker hat should have looked ridiculous on her head, what with her screaming pink caftan, but somehow she pulled it off.

"I'm not saying anything bad about full-figured women. I'm just saying I don't know if I need to look any larger than I already am," I grumbled.

"Child, you could stand to put a few pounds on," Miss Elva said. Luna and I both remained silent at that. "I mean, if you ever want to get curves like these, that is," Miss Elva shook her head sadly at what I'm sure she imagined was my poor malnourished body. I wondered what she thought of Luna, who looked like a strong wind could blow her over.

"I'm just fine with my curves, thanks," I said, scanning my phone as the text messages poured in. One from Cash caught my eye and I paused.

"Luna, I've got a text from Cash. Hold on."

"Couldn't quite stay in the background, could you?" I read out loud, narrowing my eyes at the implied criticism.

"What's that supposed to mean?" Luna demanded, her indignation seeping through the phone. "Like you purposely asked for this?"

"I have no idea. It's bulltweety is what it is. He's probably just pissed that his family knows what I do for a living now," I said, trying to dial my inner bitch back before I wrote him something I would regret.

"Don't even respond, girl. Silence is an excellent weapon," Miss Elva advised.

"God, there are like twenty things I could say to shove him in his place right now," I said, running my hands through my curls in exasperation. I slanted a look at the clock – was it too early for a drink?

"I don't think you should be drinking. What with all the press outside. You might say something stupid. That's my professional advice," Miss Elva said, reading my mind clearly.

"I wasn't going to drink. I just wondered if it was too early to drink, is all," I squinched my face up, pressing my hand to my nose.

"I'm not sure if I can even get over to your house right now. The press is camped outside the store," Luna said.

"Just stay. They'll back off eventually, I'm sure."

A banging at the door made me look up.

"Luna, I'll call you later. Just stay safe and protect yourself. Can Mathias come get you?" I spoke into the phone as I wandered warily toward the front door.

"I'll get it," Miss Elva jumped in front of me, straightening her trucker hat out, and I raised an eyebrow at her.

She swung the door wide open and I squeaked and jumped behind the door, but not before I'm sure some photographers got a shot of me. Miss Elva posed dramatically at the door.

"Oh, it's just Trace. Come in," Miss Elva said, shooing Trace inside and then pausing to smile and wave at the photographers. A few whistled at her and she chuckled and posed again, which in turn earned more applause.

"I feel like Miss Elva's brand is about to take off," Trace said with a laugh. I rolled my eyes as Miss Elva laughed and answered a few questions, being sure to show off her I Love Miss Elva hat before she swept back inside and slammed the door.

"I swear, child, I'm meant for the spotlight. I don't know why I've been hiding out for so long. Oh wait, yeah I do." Miss Elva held a finger to her lips. "I'm too much for the spotlight. I don't know if they can handle all this."

I silently agreed. Especially if the public got any wind of Miss Elva's true magickal abilities.

"Speaking of handling all that," I said, "Where's Rafe?"

"I sent him out to try and check out that yacht and report back. I mean, what's the point of having a ghost if I can't have him spy for me?"

"She makes an excellent point," Trace said and I smiled at him. I wish he didn't look so damn cute all the time. My heart sighed a little. He'd thrown on a loose long-sleeve grey t-shirt with the sleeves pushed up to reveal his tattoos, and had on cargo shorts. He'd showered since I'd seen him, and his hair was loose, just beginning to curl a little as it dried. I sort of wanted to run my hands through it.

"What are you doing here?" I asked, smiling at him.

Okay, so I was a little bit happy he had come over. There was something comforting about having him there. Like we were all on the same team. I immediately wondered why it hadn't felt that way with Cash. Maybe because I was worried he was constantly judging me? With Trace, there was no judgment because he had known us all for so long that very little surprised him. For example, he'd barely blinked when Miss Elva had mentioned her pirate ghost.

I mean, you kind of had to give a guy credit for taking Miss Elva as she was and never questioning her.

"What?" Trace asked, and I realized I'd just been gazing mindlessly at him as I thought about all the things I actually did like about him.

"Nothing," I said, turning to hide the blush that I was sure tinged my cheeks. I caught Miss Elva's look, though, and glared at her. She chuckled softly and went back to scanning her iPhone.

"Would you look at this? I'm trending again!" Miss Elva said and showed me her phone. Sure enough, there she was in her pink caftan and trucker hat, with the tagline 'America's Sweetheart.'

"America's Sweetheart? Isn't that a little..." I trailed off as I saw Miss Elva's raised eyebrow.

"Isn't that what?"

"Great? Isn't that just great?"

Trace snorted and I held back a smile as I moved to make another pot of coffee. It looked like we were going to be holed up here for a while.

"Hank, buddy, how are you?" Trace crouched and patted down an ecstatic Hank. I always forgot how much

Hank loved Trace. Now I wondered if I should have paid more attention to that in the past. Geez, what was wrong with me? I had a gazillion reporters camped out on my front porch and all I could think about was the sexy man currently sending my dog into fits of ecstasy on the floor.

Was it wrong to be jealous of my dog?

Chapter Twenty-Six

THE REST OF the morning passed essentially the same way, with my phone exploding with messages and phone calls, and repeated requests for interviews. Miss Elva continued to trend and was now lining up her own interviews. I began to wonder if I'd need a publicist for my pseudo-publicist.

"I'm going on Chelsea Handler!" Miss Elva proclaimed, and even I paused at that one.

"You've got to be kidding me," I exclaimed. I was lounging on one end of the couch, my feet stretched out, with Trace on the other, his legs stretched out next to mine. It was cozy, friendly, and not really all that sexy – yet now that the thought had been introduced in my head, all I wanted him to do was woo me all over the couch.

"Yup, I just confirmed it. Next week! They'll fly me out and everything. I'd better get to branding some hats, t-shirts, and some other stuff. What do you think? Flasks?"

"What about caftans? I mean, you pretty much live in

them. You could partner with someone and make some crazy patterns."

"I knew I kept you around for a reason," Miss Elva said, "Imma call my cousin Shelly in Miami. She's connected, if you know what I mean."

I met Trace's eyes and shrugged at the question there. With Miss Elva, 'connected' could mean anything from the mob to voodoo priests. Who was to say? I'd learned long ago not to question certain things with her.

"I've contacted the marina to see if they have any registration records for Marigold's Madness, but they won't release any information. I'm guessing too many inquiries from too many interested parties at the moment," Trace said.

"Miss Elva, whatever happened with Nico? Think we could ask him if he knows anyone named Marigold?"

"Child, he's back in Brooklyn. Doing Lord knows what, but he was let go from his job anyway because Pharma Boy was kidnapped on his watch."

"That's a bummer." I felt kind of bad for Nico, but at the same time he'd also dragged me into a whole bunch of shit that I hadn't wanted to be involved in, so my sympathy only extended so far.

"Give me a little time. I suspect I can ask around some crew guys who'll know who's who," Trace waved it away. He was right, crew people did talk to each other and all of the yachties would chatter about who was who on their charter – unless they'd signed an NDA, but typically they would still name who the clients were.

"Have they released any more details on Victoria?" I hated to ask it, but it had been bothering me all day long. I wished one of us had been there to hold her hand and tell her it would all be okay once things blew over. I also hoped whoever was responsible for making the information about Victoria public would be held accountable as an accessory to her death. Even though it was self-inflicted, there was a part of me that craved justice on her and her unborn baby's behalf.

"She slit her wrists in the bathtub. That's all I know. They didn't find her in time." Miss Elva shook her head. "It's a damn shame too. Such a waste of a young life to be lived."

Nothing more had been posted on the blog that day since I'd been thrown to the reporters. I couldn't help but think that the man that I had blown a kiss to on the yacht had been responsible for revealing my identity. I didn't believe in coincidences. I said as much to Miss Elva and Trace.

"Child, I was thinking the same damn thing. We were getting too close and they wanted to head us off," Miss Elva nodded at me as she continued to tap away on her iPhone, probably planning her world domination tour.

"And now we're barricaded in the house and can't investigate further," I added.

"Well, that they know of," Miss Elva chuckled. I knew she was talking about her magick – and Rafe, of course. We still hadn't heard from the ghost and I wondered what the heck he'd gotten up to.

Another knock at the door whipped Hank into a tizzy, and Miss Elva checked her makeup in the mirror before she swept the door open and posed. It would be annoying if it weren't so damn funny, I thought, as I watched her call out a couple of reporters who had gotten too cozy on my front porch.

"Thanks, boo, you're a doll." Miss Elva blew a kiss and came back in with two bags of food that I immediately recognized as take-out from Lucky's. Leave it to Beau to still take care of me in the midst of the madness.

"I swear to god I'd marry Beau if he were straight," I exclaimed as I unpacked the bags of food on my counter. The scent of grease and salt made my mouth water as I unpacked freshly crisped French fries, burgers, and a Reuben for Trace. I arranged all the food neatly on plates, tossed a fry to a wiggling Hank, and headed for the couch again.

I wasn't one of those people who had to eat at the dinner table, and though I had a dining room table, more often than not it collected various packages, boxes, and miscellaneous prints and pictures that I kept meaning to put away. I suppose you could call it my junk table.

We ate in silence, enjoying the comfort food, and I'd barely finished my burger when there was a knock on the door again. From the increased din outside, I had to assume this visitor was going to be someone more official.

I wasn't expecting it to be the wife.

She breezed right past Miss Elva with barely a nod and coolly assessed me where I sat on the couch, my empty plate on my lap.

"Miss Rose?"

I mean, duh, she obviously knew who I was.

"Mrs. Harrington?" I said, inflecting my voice to be as starchy and upper crust as hers. I saw her flinch slightly at the name and made a mental note of that.

She looked as casually rich as she had when I'd seen her on TV the day before. Clad in a linen sheath, with more chunky gold jewelry and what I believed had to be an actual real-life Birkin bag on her arm, she exuded an aura of old money.

I immediately disliked her. And not because of the money. There was something in her eyes that bothered me. Deciding against getting up, I leaned forward and put my plate on the table in front of me and leaned back to cross my arms across my chest.

"Ah, yes, I'm assuming you know I'm Chadwick's wife, Laura Harrington," Laura bit out, and I nodded.

"Yes, I'm aware."

Laura looked from Trace to Miss Elva and then back to me. "Is there somewhere we can talk in private?"

Miss Elva sniffed and I bit back a smile.

"These are my esteemed colleagues. You're welcome to speak freely in front of them, as I'll just tell them everything you say anyway," I smiled brightly, full bitch mode activated.

"I thought psychics were supposed to operate under a client privilege of sorts. Like a confidentiality clause? Isn't that what your website states?" Laura raised her chin at me and lightly ran her hand over the strap of her Birkin bag and I wondered if she was subtly trying to remind me how much money she had, or if it was an unconscious habit.

"You're not my client," I pointed out, my smile wide on my face.

She stiffened at that. "Of course. Naturally, I can pay you for your services." She went to reach into her purse and I held my hand up to stop her.

"I'm not taking on new clients right now. I'm booked for at least six months if not more." I smiled at her again because every time I smiled at her, she seemed to get angrier and angrier.

"Well, I'm quite sure in extenuating circumstances you can waive that and take on a new client," Laura scoffed.

I raised an eyebrow at her, delighted by the situation.

"Well, now, that certainly presents a problem. You see, you wanted me to make certain that I upheld my ethics when it came to client confidentiality, yet in almost the same breath you've now asked me to relax my standards and skip you to the head of my client list. Seems to me you want me to play fast and loose with my rules and ethics… for what, exactly? I'm not quite certain why you are here."

I watched Laura's pretty face turn an interesting shade of mottled red before she sucked in a breath.

"As I'm sure you're well aware," Laura said, her voice dripping with sarcasm, "my husband has been abducted. As you were one of the last people who spoke with him, I'd like to know if you have any details or information you can give."

"I'm not sure what that has to do with hiring me? I've already given my statement to the police," I lied. I'd meant to, but Chief Thomas was too busy to get to my statement yet. But he knew I would have told him anything that he needed to know to help him out. I wanted this mess to be over as much as everyone else who lived in Tequila Key did.

"I would greatly appreciate it if you could use – " she waved her hand in a circle at my head – "those little powers of yours to find my husband and end this mess so we can all move on."

"Victoria can't move on," I said, my eyes trained on hers.

Her lips pressed into a thin line and she nodded once, as though she was dismissing something disagreeable.

"Yes, well, that's an unfortunate byproduct of this mess," Laura said, her voice clipped as she continued to run her hand over the strap of her Birkin. I began to wonder if Birkin was a sort of safety blanket for her.

"That's an interesting choice of words," Miss Elva said, and Laura flinched at being addressed by a woman wearing a caftan and a trucker hat.

"I can't imagine you expect me to be terribly distressed over my husband's lover," Laura shrugged one shoulder as if to say, what was one life anyway?

"I'm surprised you're even interested in finding him. It doesn't seem to me like you're all that much in love with him." I decided to call it like I saw it and waited to see her response.

Again, the lips pressed thin, a stroke of the Birkin strap, and this time she glanced to the ceiling.

"Obviously, you have to understand how I'm feeling after a week such as I've had. Between Chadwick's distressing press regarding the drug prices, his abduction, and all the distasteful details that have been splashed across that awful website, well, yes, I can't say that I'm all that delighted with my husband."

In theory it was a correct answer. Except I was a hundred percent certain that I'd seen a flash of glee in her eyes when she mentioned the website.

"Obviously you have to understand that after your husband's security detail held a gun to my head and threatened my life if I didn't find him, I'm not particularly interested in getting involved any further. Quite frankly, this is your problem – not mine." At this point I was quite simply disgusted with her.

And let's be honest – nobody likes being spoken to like "the help."

"You're refusing to help me?" Laura was clearly not used to not getting her way.

"Correct."

"I can pay handsomely," Laura pointed out. Again, a stroke of the Birkin bag.

"Your money is no good here." A part of me laughed inside. I'd kind of always wanted to use that line on someone, and now I had. It couldn't have been a more perfect time or place to use it either.

"I see," Laura stiffened. "I'll just see myself out then."

"Oh, allow me," Miss Elva said graciously, sweeping to the door and opening it wide. She waved at the reporters, who all cheered for her. When Laura walked through the door, Miss Elva held a thumbs-down sign behind her back and the reporters all laughed. Laura shot a glance over her shoulder, but Miss Elva just smiled at her sweetly before shutting the door smartly in her face.

"What a bitch," Miss Elva said.

"She's in on it."

Chapter Twenty-Seven

"HOW CAN YOU BE CERTAIN?" Trace asked me after I'd stopped pacing the room, Hank following my every step.

"Hmmm, child, I don't know about all that. I mean, she's awful and a total snob, but I didn't read her involvement at all," Miss Elva said, peering out the front window and blowing kisses to her adoring public. She had a Facebook fan page already that was growing by the thousands every minute. I'd followed her too. Miss Elva was funny as all hell.

"I saw a glimmer of excitement when she talked about *that awful website*," I said, taking a sip of coffee. Not that I needed more coffee, as I was totally wired, but it was in front of me.

"Yeah, but I don't think she really loves Chadwick. And I can't say I blame her, after the way he's treated her – and, well, the rest of humanity – so maybe it's fun for her to see him get his comeuppance, get what I'm saying?" Miss Elva said.

I had to pause for a moment at her use of 'come-uppance.'

"Was that, like, on your word-of-the-day calendar or something?" I asked, tilting my head at her.

"Don't you forget how brilliant I am, missy." Miss Elva shook her head at me and then filmed me briefly.

"What are you doing?"

"I'm Snapchatting you being dismissive of my intelligence."

"Hey! I'm not the enemy here."

"You're right, I'm sorry. I understand you're under some stress here. I'll delete it."

"I'm telling you – the wife is involved. I feel it," I insisted and Miss Elva shook her head.

"I'm not seeing it. But we can err on the side of caution. So if she is, what was her point in coming here?"

"Maybe she wanted to see how much you guys knew? Or if you'd be able to find out more details with your reading?" Trace asked. He came to stand behind me and began to massage my shoulders gently. I almost whimpered in relief, as I have a tendency to carry all my tension in my neck. His thumbs worked in soothing circles, and some of the ache eased.

"I think she was putting on an act for the press, and she wanted to see how much we knew, or could find out," I said, leaning in to Trace's hands. His massage was beginning to stir up other feelings, and none of them had the least bit to do with relaxing – though they certainly would ease some tension.

"What would be the purpose of her doing that, though? If she really believed in psychics, she'd know that we could read right through her," Miss Elva pointed out.

"She thinks we're hacks. Are you kidding me? Did you see her look of distaste when she sized us up? Yeah, Mrs. Harrington is dead certain we're frauds. But she's capitalizing on the press being outside." I tried not to moan as Trace's hands worked out a particularly tight knot in my neck.

"I'm thinking maybe I need to leave you two alone," Miss Elva said, eying us from across the room.

"Oh, stop," I said, immediately blushing a bit.

"Please do. I'll be sure to take care of Althea," Trace said, and I felt my whole body flush with heat.

"This isn't a date," I pointed out, stepping away from his magical hands and glaring at him. "I thought you were going to woo me."

"We can't go anywhere, I'll have to woo from here," Trace said, a wicked smile lighting his face.

"That's my cue," Miss Elva said, gathering her bag and pulling her hat to a jaunty angle.

"Wait, where are you going?" My nerves kicked up as I realized she was about to leave me and Trace alone together.

"I'm going to find Rafe. And talk to my fans. I can't just hide out here all day, you know. My people need me." And with that, Miss Elva swept outside to the cheers of the press.

"'Her people'? How has this turned into a stage for her?" I wondered out loud.

"Because she's Miss Elva and she's awesome. I'm surprised she hasn't developed a following long before this," Trace said, leaning against the counter, his arms crossed casually over his chest.

"How long do you think I'll have to stay hidden out here?" I asked.

"Hopefully long enough that I can convince you to take a chance on me."

Chapter Twenty-Eight

I'M NOT SAYING Trace's words didn't excite me – but they also made me feel like I was standing naked in front of an auditorium of people I knew. I wasn't quite sure which emotion would win out – excitement or fear.

"That was not quite the response I was hoping for," Trace said, studying my face carefully.

I swallowed past the lump in my throat and smiled brightly at him – though I'm certain it came off as slightly maniacal. Trace barked out a laugh, then straightened, walking toward me as I just stood there, frozen to the spot with worry about what would happen between us if we took things a step further.

"Thea, it's just me. Relax," Trace said softly as he ran his hands up and down my arms. His hands left little trails of heat and I found myself leaning slightly into him, craving his closeness.

"Yeah, but it's you, Trace. You're one of my best friends. Aren't you worried about losing that?" I whispered as his arms came around me and pulled me close so I could nestle into his chest.

"Why would we lose that?"

I pulled back a little to look up at his face.

"Because if we screw up the dating part of it, won't it be tough to go back to being just friends?"

Trace smiled down at me and leaned down just enough to brush his lips softly across mine – once, twice, and once more. I felt a little swirl of delight move through me at his touch, but the nerves still remained.

"Why don't we make a pact that if we royally screw up dating each other, we'll promise to go back to being friends? Even if the friend thing is rocky for a bit."

I thought about it for a moment and then nodded.

"How about we promise to do our best to not knowingly hurt the other?" I asked, feeling we could at least honor that.

"I can wholeheartedly agree to that," Trace said, his smile flashing in his handsome face. "I never want to hurt you. You know how much I care about you."

"I care about you too," I said.

Trace tugged me across the room until we stood at the bottom of the stairs.

"I think about you. All the time. I think about how much I love diving with you, and how easily we work together on the boat or underwater. I love grabbing a drink with you at Lucky's, and I'm eager to tell you about new clients or business ideas. My mouth goes dry every time you slip out of your wetsuit – and the night of the Valentine's Day party has been seared into my brain ever since. I relive it every night while I lie in bed alone, aching for you to be in my arms again. It was one of the best and worst nights of my life, and I'm hoping that, moving forward, it will only be the best nights, so long as I can spend them with you."

I'm certain my mouth was hanging open at this point, as this was the most heartfelt and revealing thing I'd ever heard Trace say. One thing I did know is that when a man gifts you with his vulnerability, you must take care with it. I slid my arms up so they circled his neck, and met his eyes.

"I've thought about you as well. I've tried not to. I didn't want to like you or think about you or dream about you. You scare me – this scares me. Because it could actually be something more and I'm not sure how to handle that."

"Why don't we see if we can figure it out together?" Trace asked and I nodded, quite literally at a loss for words as my heart did a little spin in my chest.

Trace captured my lips in a kiss that seared me straight to my core, the promise of what could be so achingly real and close that I stumbled against him a bit. He steadied me immediately, and without another word took my hand and led me upstairs.

And, goddess help me, I went.

Chapter Twenty-Nine

IT WAS HARD to keep the smile off my face later that afternoon. A well-loved woman is a happy woman, I thought as I pulled out shredded cheese to make a plate of nachos for a whistling Trace who sat at the counter and scanned my laptop.

"Laura is on all the news sites for visiting you. Here: 'Sources say local psychic Althea Rose is expected to assist Laura Harrington in her search for her abducted husband,'" Trace read, and I rolled my eyes as I poured chips onto a plate.

"I'm telling you – she's involved. And they didn't want me looking anymore, so what better way to keep me contained than blocking me off in this house with the press?"

"Why do you say 'they' and not just her?" Trace asked, and I paused at that.

"Because it just feels like there's more than one person involved. I mean, between how they abducted Chadwick, the running of the website, and all the ins and outs of this – there has to be more than one person."

"It makes sense. So if it is the wife – what's her motive? She already has his money."

"Love," I said automatically and then tried to figure out where that had come from.

"Love? For him? She didn't seem to think too highly of him."

"Love for someone else. I'm not totally getting who or what though. Whether it's for the love of, say, a child, or a romantic love. But love is the driving force for whatever she's doing right now." I shook cheese out on top of the chips and opened a can of sliced black olives.

"Then we need to dig a little deeper," Trace said, leaning over and snagging an olive from the top of the plate.

"Hey!"

"It's one olive," Trace smiled and I found myself smiling right back at him. Things felt relaxed with him. Maybe it was post-coital glow, but it certainly felt different than with Cash. It was as though we'd just fallen into an easy rhythm.

"I'm going to throw the ball for Hank for a bit, he needs to have a good run," Trace said and I smiled to myself again as I continued to fuss over the nachos. Love me, love my dog, I thought as I sliced up a green pepper, then paused. Did I love Trace? I mean, I automatically did because he was my friend, and I certainly loved my friends. But was I in love with him?

That was a question for another day, I thought, as Miss

Elva blew through the front door in a whirlwind of sparkles and chatter.

"Good, I'm glad y'all ain't still up in the bedroom. I've got a lot to discuss with you," Miss Elva said without preamble, and I raised an eyebrow at her as I took in the outfit change.

She'd gone full sparkle this time and I could only imagine that she had blinded the photographers when the flashes bounced off the rainbow-colored sequins in a cacophony of color that covered her caftan. She had a new trucker hat on, this one also done in sequins, with the I Heart Miss Elva outlined in gold.

It was kind of like staring directly into the sun.

"Holy hell, woman, you're blinding."

"I figure I gotta get my diva on. My public demands it."

I bit my tongue at that and slid the plate of nachos into the microwave. Snagging a Corona from the fridge for Miss Elva, I began to pull leaves from a little mint plant I had in a dish over the sink. It was the one plant I managed to keep alive and I wasn't going to think too deeply on the fact that its primary use was to flavor my drinks.

"Are you trying to burn holes into their eyes?"

"Don't you be getting your sass on with me. I figured you'd be in a better mood after your afternoon with Trace," Miss Elva said, dropping into one of the stools that lined my counter and taking a swig from her bottle of beer.

"I am in a good mood. I won't lie about that. But I'm also ready for this house arrest to be over so I can go about my life," I said, clapping my hands over the mint leaves to release the flavor.

Miss Elva leaned dangerously back to glance out my back door, and I cringed as the stool creaked. I wasn't sure what I would do if she toppled off, but I guarantee I'd be taking a picture of it for her social media.

"So? Was it as good as I thought it could be? I swear there were sparks bouncing off the two of you. It was getting so hot in here I had to step out or I was going to get singed."

I glanced out back to see Trace running around with Hank and then cleared my throat. I found myself blushing for a moment and Miss Elva let out a hoot of laughter and slapped the counter.

"Child, I haven't seen you tongue-tied in a while." Miss Elva chuckled and took another swig of her beer. "That's when you know you're doing it right."

"Oh, yeah, it was all right, that's for sure. In so many ways," I admitted, a smile breaking out on my face as I began to build my mojito. The microwave dinged and I slid the plate of nachos out and in front of Miss Elva. As though he had a sixth sense for food, Trace wandered inside.

"Yum, I'm starving," Trace said, nodding at Miss Elva as he sat next to her. I slid him a beer. It was all very cozy and easy and I tried not to reflect on the fact that this is exactly how my life and my relationships should be.

Hot in the bedroom, easy in everyday life.

Yeah, okay, I could maybe get used to this. We just needed to get Chadwick home, the press could move on, and I could go back to my happy existence of diving and reading tarot cards.

It shouldn't be that hard, right?

We all turned as the door opened and Hank skittered across the room to greet the newest visitor.

"Luna! How'd you get out of the shop?"

Luna somehow looked as stunning as usual, barely a hair out of place, her elegant grey sheath dress unwrinkled. Crystals sparkled at her ears and wrists, and she carried a large winter-white leather tote. Obediently, she bent to pat a wriggling Hank and then smiled at us. She paused for a moment, her eyes sliding between Trace and me before shooting me a nearly imperceptible look.

It didn't take my friends long to figure things out.

"Mathias slipped me out the back door of the shop and then muscled me up the front steps here."

"He didn't want to come in?" I was already opening a bottle of white wine for Luna.

"He's got an ER shift tonight. He does a few rotations a month to help out."

Luna's boyfriend was an urgent care doctor and hot as all get-out. I couldn't have asked for a better man for her. Not only did he accept her exactly as she was – white witch powers and all – but he was over the moon for her. That's all you can really ask for.

"Have you heard anything new?"

"I saw that Laura was here earlier today. You helping her find Chadwick now?" Luna said, settling herself on a stool and studying the plate of nachos carefully. Having finally decided on the perfect chip, she slid it from the plate and nibbled delicately on a corner.

"Nope, but I'm fairly convinced she's in on it." I relayed what had happened during our meeting to bring Luna up to speed.

"And you're certain she's involved."

"Yes."

Luna thought for a moment, then glanced back toward the front of the house where the press was still camped outside.

"I think we'll have to do some magickal exploration then. Since our physical movements are limited."

"What are you suggesting?" Miss Elva asked, her sequins flashing as she reached for a nacho.

"I'd say a dreamwalk or an astral projection. No?" Luna asked.

"Hmm, I haven't done a dreamwalk in a while. That could be fun," Miss Elva said and I saw Trace smile.

"Y'all are crazy. And I love you for it. Tell me what a dreamwalk is – basically what it sounds like, right?" Trace asked.

"We're just as crazy as you, Trace, for hanging out with us," Luna said easily and Trace laughed, holding his hands up in mock defense.

"I never said I wasn't crazy. It's why we all get along."

"Dreamwalking is essentially visiting someone in their sleep – in their dreams. You can talk to them, walk with them in their dreams, and glean bits of information as needed," Miss Elva explained.

Trace looked slightly taken aback. "That's kind of a powerful tool, no?" he asked.

"All magick is a powerful tool. It's why we swear oaths to harm no one," Luna said, and Trace nodded.

"With great power comes great responsibility?" he said, quoting Spiderman or one of those superhero movies that I could never remember.

"Exactly."

"Remind me to never piss you ladies off," Trace said, shooting me a quick smile.

"Yeah, I haven't sworn an oath actually… so be careful, buddy," I said, and Trace laughed at me. I loved how easy it was to joke with him about this stuff and know that I wasn't being judged.

"Who do we dreamwalk then?" I asked, directing my question at Luna and Miss Elva.

"Chadwick," they said together, which came as a surprise to me.

"Why him? Why not the wife?"

"Because he'll be able to reveal his surroundings and show us the face of who took him," Luna said. I supposed that made sense, though I had little interest in getting inside Chadwick's twisted brain.

"Can I just ask what your plan is after you find out who took him?" Trace asked.

"We'll tell Chief Thomas," I said immediately.

"Don't you think he'll wonder how you know?" Trace asked, an incredulous expression on his face.

"I mean, I think he's kind of used to us knowing stuff at this point. He's seen some of what we're capable of, anyway," I said.

"Yeah, but he's got the FBI involved. It's a whole different ballgame with the Feds."

Huh, I hadn't thought about that. I looked at Miss Elva and Luna. "What do we do with the information? Are we going to let the people who took him get away?"

"What if we're able to make it so Chadwick lowers the price of the drug – I mean, isn't that the goal of the people who kidnapped him? If we can somehow ensure that, do the kidnappers need to face justice? Maybe we can let them off for the greater good," Luna asked.

"I feel like that's getting into very murky waters, ethically," I said.

"Why don't we just gather information for now and then see what we want to do with it?" Miss Elva said, and we all nodded.

"What has to be done for a dreamwalk?" I asked.

"I need to charge my crystals and get a few things together," Luna nodded toward her tote.

"We just need my spell and a bit of this and that," Miss Elva said.

"And we do this when?"

Luna and Miss Elva looked at me like I was out of my damn mind.

"Um, at night. When people are sleeping. You know, to get in his dreams."

Right, got it.

Chapter Thirty

A FEW HOURS later we were all set up for our dreamwalk. Well, at least I assumed we were, as I actually had no clue on what was needed for one, nor did I understand any protocol regarding this procedure. Procedure? Spell? Ritual?

See? I was kind of at a loss. I'm surprised my friends trust me with these things. Last time I messed up a spell, I brought Rafe through the veil.

"Hey, where's Rafe? Aren't you worried?"

Miss Elva shrugged. She'd set up some crystals and a small silver bowl in front of her. We were all sitting on the bed in my guest room. Though Miss Elva said she preferred doing this outside, we had decided that with the press hanging around, we'd best keep it under wraps inside.

Though I kind of thought Miss Elva wouldn't mind being photographed doing something fantastical. She had her following to please, after all.

"So what's the plan then?"

"You and I will walk and Luna will hold the spell," Miss Elva said and I blinked at her.

"I'm dreamwalking? I have no idea how to dreamwalk," I said, stating what was already readily obvious.

"That's why you've got a chaperone," Luna said, rolling her eyes as she pointed at Miss Elva.

"Sequins McFabulous over here is my chaperone? Yeah, that's going to go well," I grumbled.

"Watch yourself or I'll kick your ass into another dimension," Miss Elva threatened.

Trace straightened. "Hey, now, I don't like that. You better not put her in harm's way," he said, glaring at Miss Elva. She patted his knee gently.

"Don't you worry, loverboy. The whole point of me going along is to keep this one out of trouble," Miss Elva said, nodding at me.

"Who says I would get in trouble?" Everyone on the bed looked at me in disbelief. "Well, fine then. If I'm such a screw-up, why am I even going?"

"Because some of your powers are more suited to this than mine," Luna said smoothly.

"Oh." I was still discovering that I had more magick than I had originally been led to believe. My mother, a world-renowned psychic, had failed to mention that I also carried some extra other-worldly powers. Luna was still miffed at her for that, and was slowly taking me under her tutelage in order to test where my strengths lay.

"What's going to happen is that we'll begin the ritual, and get you and Miss Elva into a trance-like state. Once you're there, Miss Elva will help guide you and you'll go visit Chadwick in his dreams. Right now, we're establishing this room as a safe chamber of sorts, so you'll feel comfortable traveling away from your physical body."

"Um," Trace said, clearly bothered by that concept.

"Trace, it helps that you're here, because Althea will feel safe knowing that you're on hand to protect her physical wellbeing," Luna said smoothly. I immediately saw that she had said the right thing. The tension in Trace's shoulders eased a bit and he gave a sharp nod of assent.

I swear, tell a guy to be a protector and he all but salutes. It's ingrained in their very DNA, I think.

"Okay, so, trance, walk to Chadwick's dreams – then what? Interrogate him? Shine the bright light in his face and beat him with a bat?" I was only half-kidding. I really didn't like Chadwick.

"Information gathering only, Thea," Miss Elva said gently. "And, perhaps some powers of persuasion. I'm going to test him and see how suggestible his mind is. From what I've gathered being around him, I suspect his mind will be easily led."

"I'll let you do the talking," I said, again only half-kidding. I often found that, if left to my own devices, my lack of a filter got me in trouble.

"We all good on this, then?" Luna asked, checking her watch. It was nearly eleven at night, and we'd all had a long day. We'd wanted to wait long enough to ensure that Chadwick would most likely be sleeping.

"Yes," I said, then started when Trace grabbed me and kissed me once – hard.

"I've got you, Thea," Trace said. I smiled at him, patting his cheek gently in reassurance. Miss Elva and I both stretched out on the bed, holding hands, and Luna began to set up the circle of protection around us.

I let my mind wander as Luna called upon the goddess and the elements for protection, just allowing myself to feel safe in this moment, and trying not to laugh at the fact that I was lying on the bed, holding hands with Glitter Bomb next to me. I'd sort of gotten used to expecting the unexpected in my life these days.

"The circle is set. I'll now lead you into a deep meditative state," Luna said, her voice soft as she began a ritual incantation that would lead Miss Elva and me deep into our minds and through a door into another realm.

I didn't even have time to be surprised by how quickly I found myself standing in an empty room of sorts. It wasn't really a room, as there were no walls – it was just a space. A safe space in the middle of nowhere – maybe 'the space between' would be the best way to describe it. In seconds, Miss Elva materialized beside me.

"Where are we?"

"A holding spot. Until we direct where we want to go," Miss Elva explained, her sequins shimmering as she grabbed my hand again. She spoke softly beneath her breath, then there was a soft whishing sound and in seconds we were sitting in another bedroom.

This one was far different than my guest bedroom, though. First of all, there was a lot of black leather and red silk. The entire theme of the room was black on black on black, with lots of mirrors and flashes of red. After my mind got over the initial shock of so much leather, I realized that we were in some kind of sex den. I nearly rolled my eyes, but then I caught sight of Chadwick.

"Ew," I whispered. His skinny body was done up in innumerable leather straps and bindings, and he was tied to the bed. A hard-muscled man was currently slapping his face gently with a tasseled whip.

Miss Elva turned and raised an eyebrow at me. This was certainly a new development. I had known that Chadwick certainly liked his mistresses, but had been unaware that he also liked the misters.

"You're dismissed," Miss Elva said clearly and Chadwick started. The man holding the tasseled whip nodded immediately and wandered from the room. Presumably to go dominate someone else in another chamber, for all I knew. Chadwick glared at us both.

"What are you two doing here?"

"It doesn't seem to me like you're all that distraught about getting kidnapped," Miss Elva said, settling herself onto a corner of the bed. Chadwick was still restrained, and I realized the beauty of the situation. He had nowhere to run unless he woke up or one of us or his Dominant untied him.

"I'm escaping. Being kidnapped is boring," Chadwick said, shrugging as much as he could in the restraints. I said nothing.

"You aren't bothered about being abducted?"

"My security will find me. I pay them too much not to. Once I'm out everyone will think I'm a hero for surviving. It's only going to be good for business," Chadwick said, unconcerned.

Miss Elva looked at me, surprise in her eyes. That's when I realized Chadwick clearly didn't know about the website revealing the smarmy details of his life. I watched as Miss Elva weighed how much to reveal.

And – for once in my life – I kept my mouth shut.

"Can you tell us what happened?" Miss Elva said, deciding to start there. I was surprised by how remarkably unconcerned Chadwick seemed to be with the fact that he was tied up in a sex den having a casual conversation with us. But I suppose dreams are always kind of weird – maybe this was business as usual for Chadwick.

"I don't really know. We'd been partying, you know? And I was finally making my way to my bedroom and boom – everything went black. Next thing I know, I'm tied up and gagged."

"Did you see who hit you?"

"No. I told you, everything went black," Chadwick said, rolling his eyes.

"Well, obviously you're being kept alive. Who's feeding you?" Miss Elva said patiently, though I saw her forehead crease with annoyance.

"I don't know. The door opens and food gets tossed in. Like I'm a wild animal or something." Chadwick scoffed. "Clearly they're afraid of me and my strength. Only a coward would hide behind a door like that."

At this point it was taking every last bit of restraint I had not to bust out laughing. Clearly Chadwick was a narcissist if he even remotely thought his skinny ass was anything someone would fear.

"You don't think it's because they don't want to reveal their identities to you?" Miss Elva asked smoothly.

"Nah, they're clearly scared of me. It's fine. I'll wait it out," Chadwick shrugged. "Plus, as I said, the longer I'm held, the more heroic the story will be. I'm going to be like a freakin' celebrity by the time I'm out of here. It's going to be awesome."

I saw the moment Miss Elva decided not to reveal anything about the website. It would be much more damaging to Chadwick's ego and his future if he found out after the fact.

"Can you tell me anything about where you're staying? Is it a cell?"

"I think I was on a boat for a while, because I felt the motion of the ocean, if you get me." Chadwick managed to leer, though I had no idea what for. He was clearly more interested in men than Miss Elva. "But now I think I'm on an island somewhere. At least I can still hear the waves sometimes, when they lead me to the bathroom. No windows in my room, just a bed."

"Do you hear anything when they take you to the bathroom? Voices? Does the person leading you seem taller or shorter than you? Walk softly? Seem like a woman?"

Chadwick laughed long and hard at that.

"Please, don't insult me. No woman would be able to overpower me," Chadwick said, all but crying from laughter.

Did I mention I really didn't like this man?

"Do you want our help in trying to get you out or not?" Miss Elva interrupted, finally showing her first signs of impatience. Which certainly impressed me, as I'd been studying the various instruments of domination around the room for the past few minutes and trying to decide which one I was going to use first on Chadwick. And not in a sexual way, if you get my meaning.

"Nah, I'm good. Like I said, this is going to be great for business," Chadwick said, clearly at ease with his life.

Miss Elva paused for a moment, studying her hands before straightening to lean over Chadwick until he was forced to look into her eyes.

"Chadwick Harrington, you are going to listen very closely to me, do you understand?"

"Yes," Chadwick said, his jaw slack, his eyes focused unblinking on Miss Elva's. I swear, just when I think I know all the facets of what Miss Elva's capable of, she surprises me with something else. Because I was fairly certain she'd gone and hypnotized Chadwick with just a look.

"When you get out of this predicament, you are going to realize the error of your ways. You will drop the price of the Alzheimer's drug and make it readily available to everyone. Not only will you do this willingly, but you'll even donate half of the proceeds to further Alzheimer's research. You will give your company's board of directors full say in allowing this, irrespective of the level of control you have over the company once certain things come to light. Do you understand me?"

Chadwick nodded, his eyes still wide and unblinking.

"Tell me what you're going to do when your kidnappers release you."

"I'm going to lower the price of the Alzheimer's drug so that everyone can have it," Chadwick said immediately.

"And you are going to live the rest of your life making amends for the awful things you've done," Miss Elva added.

Chadwick nodded along. "Yes. I've been a bad person. I will make amends."

"That's a good boy," Miss Elva said, patting his cheek gently and then easing herself from the bed. She walked across the room to where I stood, silently cheering her on in my head, and took my hand.

"Let's go."

The room faded away.

Chapter Thirty-One

"WHAT A PIECE OF CRAP," Miss Elva said as soon as we blinked back into my guest bedroom.

"You're back!" Trace exclaimed, reaching over to squeeze my hand.

"Let me close the circle," Luna said. Trace pulled his hand back, watching as Luna ran through the ritual of closing the circle and thanking the goddess for her protection.

Miss Elva and I both sat up once the circle was closed.

"Let's go downstairs, I feel silly sitting on the bed," I said.

Everyone tromped downstairs. My blood felt like it was humming from the adrenalin rush of the trip. It was so weird – we had been in someone else's dreams and yet our physical bodies had remained in one spot. I supposed it was something to dissect another day, as Luna and Trace were eagerly waiting for details.

"It's midnight!" I exclaimed. It hadn't seemed like we were gone all that long. Trace was already in the kitchen pouring wine and grabbing beer for us. We all settled down on the couch and I sipped the crisp white wine, letting the flavors settle on my tongue and soothe the pump of excitement that coursed through me.

"Yes, time goes much faster than you realize when you're traveling astrally," Miss Elva said.

"What did you learn?" Luna asked.

"That Chadwick is, and continues to be, a complete asshole," I said.

"He has no interest in being rescued," Miss Elva said, and filled everyone in on the encounter. I let Miss Elva lead; it was her show, after all.

"He's gay?" Trace asked, his forehead crinkling in surprise.

"He certainly seems to enjoy being dominated by men," I said.

"Huh, I wonder why all the mistresses then," Trace said, taking a swig of his beer.

"Probably to try and over-compensate? Or keep up an image?"

"Miss Elva didn't even tell you the best part," I said, smiling at her, "but she hypnotized Chadwick and insisted that he lower the price of the drug. So I'm really hoping he gets released soon – that way the drug will become readily available to everyone."

"I love you, Miss Elva," Luna said, squeezing her arm.

"Me too," Trace said, saluting her with his beer.

Miss Elva waved the compliments away, though I could tell the attention pleased her.

"I just did what anyone would have done if they had

the power to." She stood, stretching her arms above her head. "I'm beat. And we still need to find Rafe."

I kept forgetting that Rafe had been missing for a while now. Well, not missing, but gathering information. I wondered how far he had to travel to find the information he was seeking, and whether ghost travel was faster over long distances than regular travel.

"You look like you're going to fall asleep at any moment," Trace said, and I realized just how exhausted I was.

"Astral travel takes a lot out of you. I could sleep for twelve hours. I'm going home. Luna, want a lift?" Miss Elva asked.

Luna sized us up. Normally, she would have slept in my guest room. But I think she correctly assumed that Trace was going to stay the night.

"Sounds good. See you guys tomorrow," Luna said, and before you could say "I'm outta here," they were gone. I saw a few flashes go off, which meant there were still reporters camped outside.

"Let me just take Hank out quick and we can go to sleep."

I smiled as Trace took care of Hank and I cleaned up the dishes. It was decidedly cozy, and felt normal. Easy – that was the word I was looking for.

I needed more easy in my life.

Chapter Thirty-Two

"GOOD MORNING, BEAUTIFUL." Trace's lips pressed against my neck and I squirmed back against him, enjoying his arms circling me. It was decidedly comfortable, yet at the same time quite enticing.

"This is certainly a different way to start our mornings than going diving," I murmured as Trace rolled over me.

Not that I was complaining, I thought later as I showered, a smile on my lips. I lectured myself about enjoying this honeymoon period. I felt like, at the beginning of every relationship, there's this period of time where you're smitten before the sheen wears off a bit. I was determined not to polish any of the sheen off of this one, though, and just try to enjoy it for what it was, in the now.

I screeched as Trace popped his head in the shower with a cup of coffee in his hand.

"Jesus, warn a woman, would you?"

"Sorry. Luna and Miss Elva are here. More stuff on the website, and I think Rafe is back. Drink up," Trace said cheerfully, handing me the cup of coffee and slapping my butt before he whistled his way from the bathroom.

Well, then. I suppose I couldn't complain about free coffee delivery.

Downstairs, I found Luna and Miss Elva looking at my laptop and clucking their tongues. Rafe hovered in the corner, glaring at Hank.

"Rafe, good to see you," I said, though I didn't necessarily mean it.

"Devil beast is still here, I see," Rafe sneered down at where Hank tilted his head at him.

"I'm assuming that's where the ghost is?" Trace asked, pressing a kiss to my cheek as he handed me a plate of peanut butter and banana toast. I kept forgetting that Trace couldn't see Rafe, yet he readily accepted his existence.

"Yes, you can pretty much see where Rafe is because Hank follows him around the room. It freaks Rafe out, but I think it's funny," I said, blowing a smooch at Rafe as he made a very impolite gesture in my direction.

"What's on the blog today?" I asked, biting into the peanut-buttery yumminess and nodding at the computer.

"Nothing we don't already know, but it seems everyone else is freaking out about it," Miss Elva said, turning to show a picture of Chadwick done up in his leather straps and surrounded by a bevy of beautiful men.

"Ah. I wondered if that would get revealed."

"Seems that Tara girl went on a rant and had another meltdown," Miss Elva said, clicking to show me a video of the distraught mistress having a freakout. It actually made me laugh. You just can't fix stupid – and she was one of the dumbest I'd ever run across.

"When did Rafe decide to show back up? Did he find out anything worthwhile?"

"Well, Rafe? Are you going to talk?" Miss Elva said, turning to look at where the pirate ghost hovered in the corner.

"Oh, now you want to talk to me? Hmpf." Rafe stuck his nose in the air.

"He's been in a snit all morning because of all the attention I've been getting." Miss Elva rolled her eyes at me. "I've asked him several times where he's been, but he's been too busy being cranky."

"Rafe, come on, just tell us what you found out. You know Miss Elva loves you. But she deserves attention too. Just look at how beautiful she is," I crooned to the ghost.

Rafe sniffed and crossed his arms. "My lovemountain is a goddess."

"Of course she is. Which means she needs to be worshipped. So her adoring public is worshipping her, is all. She still loves you."

Rafe floated over and looked down at Miss Elva.

"Is that the truth of it? You haven't forsaken me?"

"Rafe, you should know I'd just toss you through the veil again if I was done with you." Miss Elva shook her head at him and Rafe shuddered visibly at her words.

"Please don't dismiss me," Rafe begged.

"Stop it, now, you're making a fool of yourself," Miss Elva said, smoothing her hands down her emerald green caftan.

Sequined, naturally.

Rafe immediately straightened, his nose up in the air, once again resuming his cocky pirate attitude.

"I took the mission seriously, but might have gotten slightly distracted," Rafe finally said. Miss Elva snorted, shaking her head at the ghost.

"'Distracted' is an understatement. Hooters had some sort of company-sponsored yacht, and Rafe claims he mistook their yacht for the one we actually wanted him to check out."

"It was an honest mistake," Rafe said, and I rolled my eyes.

"Sure it was, Rafe. Don't be getting all mad at Miss Elva for having a following, though, when you're busy checking out busty women on a yacht," I said, crossing my arms as I lectured the ghost.

"Hey, that's a good point. Best take care, Rafe," Miss Elva said, but I could tell she was just teasing him. We all knew Miss Elva had the upper hand in that relationship.

"It was purely for research," Rafe said.

I smiled widely at that one. "What, pray tell, does a ghost pirate research in modern-day society?"

"I was looking at all the new instruments used to command and pilot such a vast ship," Rafe said smoothly. I had to give him credit – it wasn't a bad response. Too bad I knew what a lecherous old goat he was.

"I'd say those weren't the only instruments you were looking at," I said.

Trace snorted. I knew that even though he couldn't hear Rafe, he'd gotten the gist of the conversation. "Boobs," he said, and shrugged. "Every man's downfall."

"Well, most men," I pointed out, thinking of Beau.

"Does anyone care what I did end up finding out after my extensive research?"

"Yes, Rafe, we'd be delighted if you could tell us what you saw aside from half-naked ladies," I said.

"Nathaniel's mother is named Marigold."

And this is what we would call a mic drop.

Chapter Thirty-Three

TRACE WAS ALREADY ON IT, pulling up articles on my laptop until we found out that Marigold, Nathaniel's mother, had died of early-onset Alzheimer's years ago. Nathaniel would have been just a teenager at the time – perhaps eighteen or nineteen. I wondered how long he had hated Chadwick for.

And if he was going to kill him.

The festering anger of losing a mother to a horrific disease could have made anyone do something rash – but this was so well-calculated and brilliantly executed that I had to wonder how long Nathaniel had been planning it.

"It seems so obvious. How has the FBI not figured this out yet?" I wondered, as I paced the room and debated what we should do.

"It looks like his mother was named Anna Marie Amaigo. Marigold was a nickname used by family only, according to her obituary."

I leaned over his shoulder to see a picture of a woman with blonde hair and a sunny smile – I could see why her nickname was Marigold. My heart twinged at the thought of her smile being dimmed too soon.

"What do we do? Tell Chief Thomas?" I asked, nibbling my lower lip as I worked through all the levels of what was right and wrong in this situation.

"What happens if we let it play out?" Trace asked, playing devil's advocate.

"I don't think they'll kill Chadwick. They wouldn't go through all this to embarrass him – and not tell him about it – if he wasn't meant to feel the humiliation once he's released. The entire point of As His World Burns would be moot if he didn't actually experience the embarrassment that he's meant to feel. That loss of dignity is the entire reason for all this," I said. I knew in my very soul that Chadwick was going to be released.

"So, banking on that, do we wait it out? See how this all plays out?" It wasn't like us to not take action, but the moral ground here was a little murky.

"What about Victoria? Don't you think that's on Nathaniel's hands?" Luna asked softly and I nodded.

"I do. I mean… it's on Chadwick's hands too. But the reveal is what triggered her to take her life," I said.

"I don't think anyone can actually be charged with murder when it's a suicide," Miss Elva said gently, her eyes sad. "Because it was her choice. I'm not sure if it was her destiny or not – but ultimately, it was her choice. And the police will do nothing. The only thing Nathaniel is going to get in trouble for is abducting Chadwick. And I wonder how much he'd get for that, because he tipped them off on the insider trading. I can see Nathaniel working out a sweet deal and coming out the hero in all this."

"This whole thing was brilliantly executed," Luna said, and I had to agree with her. It seemed like no matter what we did, things were going to work out exactly as Nathaniel had planned.

"So? We wait?" I turned and met my friends' eyes, one by one. They each nodded in turn and I sighed.

"We wait."

Chapter Thirty-Four

"I'M JUST GOING to take Hank out for a bit," I said, sliding my phone into my hand and motioning to Hank.

"Want company?" Trace asked.

"I'm going to try and call my mom," I said. It was a blatant lie and I didn't care. Sitting around and doing nothing in this situation felt awful.

I tossed the ball for an enthusiastic Hank, then settled into the deep corner of my outdoor couch. Scrolling through my phone, I found the number I was looking for. Nico had given it to me when I'd asked for a rundown of Chadwick's closest people.

It rang for a while, and I heard a little delay… typical of calling another country.

"Ms. Rose, I've been wondering if I would hear from you," Nathaniel said, his tone jovial through the phone. I strained to hear any other identifying sounds in the background, but he'd taken care of that. As any good security person would, I thought, and bent to pick up the soggy ball and launch it across the yard again.

"I'm sorry about your mother," I said.

There was a pause on the other end. I suspected Nathaniel had not expected me to lead with that.

"Ah, yes. Well, thank you. It was a devastating loss," Nathaniel said, his sadness still evident in his voice.

"I can only imagine. I understand what a horrible disease Alzheimer's is," I said carefully, smoothing my hand down my dress.

"Unless you've experienced it intimately, it's virtually impossible to understand the depth and difficulty of such a thing," Nathaniel said.

I found myself nodding along, then realized I should speak. "I agree. I'm sorry you've had to go through that," I said, unsure how to navigate the next bit of conversation.

"Thank you."

"Will you be releasing Chadwick soon?"

"Are you going to feed my name to the police?" Nathaniel parried back and I let that question hang for a moment.

"Here's the deal – I'm not going to say anything on a few conditions."

"It's interesting to me that you think you're in a position to ask for anything," Nathaniel chuckled. "You really have no idea the depth and breadth of my connections, as well as my security capabilities. I could have you disappear without a trace by the end of the day. Your dog as well. No record of you to even exist. I can wipe out your Social Security number, your birth certificate, and – literally – those who knew you."

"I mean, that'd be a lot of people, considering you fed me to the press and the entire nation knows about me now, but yeah, I get what you're trying to say," I said, allowing sarcasm to coat my words.

"I like you, Ms. Rose," Nathaniel said after another chuckle.

"I kind of like you, as well, if I'm being honest. But here's the problem I'm struggling with – Victoria. Someone has to be held accountable for her."

Nathaniel paused again. I tossed the ball again as I waited for his response.

"Unfortunately, the best laid plans often go astray. An unfortunate casualty, of course. I'm sorry for that, I am. Not that I liked her much, but it was certainly not my intention to push her to that point. Had I read any signs of instability or depression in her, I certainly wouldn't have done it."

"See, that's the problem when you play God. You just don't know what the ramifications of your actions will be," I said, anger whipping through me.

"And when people like Chadwick play God, millions suffer. Who is more right in the situation?"

I had no answer for that. My sliding scale of morality had no frame of reference for something like this.

"Here's what I'm going to ask for in exchange for my silence," I said, reaching up to tug a hand through my curls as I thought about what I wanted, "I'd like you to set up a memorial for Victoria, as well as some way to remember her positively, so people know more about her than just her affair with Chadwick. A center for depression and suicide awareness might be best. Funded yearly by a private anonymous donor."

Silence stretched between us and I waited to hear what he would say.

"You have yourself a deal, Ms. Rose. Despite what it may seem to you, I'm not entirely unfeeling."

"Thank you," I said softly.

"You know about me and Laura, don't you?"

I hadn't, but that fit in with my view of her being involved and doing it for love. I just hadn't known she was in love with Chadwick's best friend.

"I do," I said softly.

"I'll be taking her away. We are going to put it out that she was devastated by Chadwick's betrayal and I stepped in to support her. Naturally, we fell in love."

"Naturally," I said.

"We'll be releasing Chadwick soon. The hope is that he will see the error of his ways in regards to the drug. Otherwise, I'm going to make it so that he misses his patent deadlines and the formula goes off-patent. One way or the other, we are going to do humanity a load of good."

I didn't doubt that; I just hated that it had happened in such a manner. And how naïve was I? I could only imagine the millions of back-handed deals and hush stories when it came to large pharma companies and the money they made from things like the cancer industry.

"I should let you know that we might have done a little bit on our end to… um, convince Chadwick to lower the price."

"That's… very interesting to hear. Any way I could check to see if it worked?"

"I'd say just ask him his plans for the drug. See what he says?"

"I absolutely will do so. I'm certainly indebted to you for your assistance," Nathaniel said, and I almost laughed. This call had taken a weird turn.

"I hope you and Laura find happiness," I said, and I could tell that I had, once again, surprised him.

"I mean it, Ms. Rose. If you ever need anything, you'll be able to get a hold of me. I'll make sure of it. In the meantime, I'll be in touch in regards to the suicide prevention center. I think it's an excellent idea."

With that, the connection was cut. I looked up to see Trace poking his head out the door, his eyebrow raised in question.

"That didn't sound like your mother," Trace said, coming to sit next to me on the couch.

"No, it wasn't. I'm sorry for lying. I needed to make that call without interference." I waited for Trace to get angry at me – like Cash would have – for taking things into my own hands.

Trace reached out and threaded his fingers through mine.

"Did it work out the way you wanted it to?"

I smiled at him, feeling grateful that somehow we had stumbled our way into each other.

"I suppose as well as it could in this situation. Suffice it to say, I've made a friend in a very high place," I shrugged.

Trace leaned over to kiss me. "Think he could get me Knicks tickets?"

I laughed against his mouth, loving the easiness of being with him, and shook my head.

"I only use my power for good."

"The Knicks are good!

"Nope," I laughed, and went inside to tell the girls what had happened.

Chapter Thirty-Five

LATER THAT NIGHT a loud buzz of shouting and voices outside my door gave us pause. Miss Elva strode over and flung the door open.

"What's all this ruckus?"

"Pharma Boy's been released!"

Car doors were slamming and people were scrambling to get to wherever Chadwick was. In moments, the street in front of my house was empty once again and I was feeling positively cheerful at having my freedom back.

"Ohhhh child, they went for the low blow with this last one," Miss Elva said, looking at her phone. Trace had flipped the television on, and we watched the same perky blonde try not to smile as the video played in the background of an angry Chadwick, stumbling along, with a blanket over his shoulders and the police at his side.

"Is he naked?"

"Mmmhmm. Look at this. They can't show that on the news, but the picture is everywhere," Miss Elva said, holding up her phone. We all crowded around.

"Oh my," Luna said, covering her mouth with her hand.

Chadwick stood front and center on As His World Burns, without a stitch of clothing on. A large black arrow, in what looked to be duct tape, ran down his stomach and pointed at his decidedly small package.

"That's cold-blooded right there," Trace said, letting out a low whistle.

"How'd he get so many mistresses?" Luna wondered.

"Money," I said automatically.

"It's clearly not for anything he was bringing to the table. I've had tater tots bigger than that," Miss Elva said.

I closed my eyes and counted to five.

Nope, I was still going to laugh.

"Chadwick Harrington was recovered unharmed on a lifeboat today in the ocean outside Tequila Key. No word yet on any information about his abductors. It's been said that Mr. Harrington will release a statement shortly after the authorities question him. It should be noted that Mr. Harrington has been brought into custody in regards to the insider trading allegations. His lawyers will be meeting with him shortly," the blonde woman said cheerfully.

"I sincerely hope his statement has to do with lowering the price of the Alzheimer's drug. It's the only way he's going to come out of this looking remotely like a good person," I said.

"If I'm as good at what I do as I think I am, that's exactly what will be happening," Miss Elva sniffed.

"Yeah, my lovemountain is the boss lady of everything that is awesome," Rafe said, and Miss Elva blew him a kiss.

"And that certainly didn't take long." The blonde listened to her microphone for a second before looking at the camera again. "Chadwick Harrington has just released a statement that the price of the drug will be lowered, effective immediately, in order to make it available to everyone who is suffering from Alzheimer's."

We all cheered. I couldn't help but feel like this was a win, by nefarious means or not. Nathaniel was right, all of humanity would benefit from this.

And that's one thing I've learned – you must celebrate the wins in life.

Epilogue

THE SUN JUST creased the horizon, its rays shooting out across the light chop of the waves that slapped the hull of the dive boat. Trace and I were heading out to one of our favorite dive spots. It had been too long since we'd dived together and we were both itching to get wet.

I looked over at where Trace manned the wheel. He glanced up at me, his teeth flashing white in his face.

I was still surprised to be standing here, next to him – not just as my friend, but as my lover. It was easy and it felt good. I decided, for once in my life, to just let things be and not question it too much. Maybe living in the now wasn't such a bad thing after all.

"Miss Elva said Rafe made contact with Victoria," I said over the sound of the boat.

Trace smiled. "One of these days you're going to need to draw me a picture of Rafe so I can get the image in my head," he said.

"I will. Or maybe Miss Elva can make it so you can

see him. Since he doesn't seem to be going anywhere anytime soon, you might as well be able to see him."

"That'd be badass," Trace said in awe, and I laughed again.

"He said Victoria is happy. She's moved on to a better place and there doesn't seem to be any lingering feelings of dissonance or anger. So, I guess that's something. He told her about the Victoria Lavish Center for Suicide Prevention and she seemed really pleased, he said."

"That's really good to hear. I know that was a tough part of this whole situation for you."

I shrugged. It was, but I've also learned that there is only so much I can control. And for now, my happiness was in my control. I went over and leaned against Trace and he looped an arm around my shoulders.

"This is nice," Trace said, pressing a kiss to my head.

I could use some nice in my life.

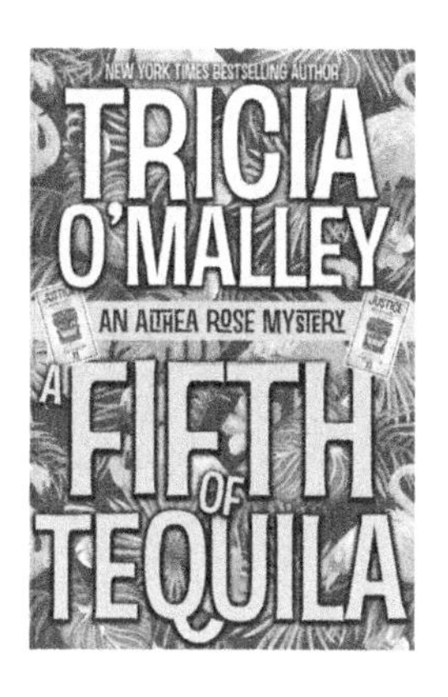

The following is an excerpt from A Fifth of Tequila

Book 5 in the Althea Rose Mystery Series

Chapter One

I'VE NEVER WANTED to be famous. I'm happy to leave that particular joy to my mother, the incomparable psychic to the stars, Abigail Rose. With fame comes a level of responsibility and attention to personal detail that I'm just not interested in maintaining.

As evidenced by my best friend, Beau, sighing and handing me a napkin over the smooth wood top of the bar he owned.

"Mustard," Beau said, pointing to where a splotch of yellow had dripped onto my pretty blue sundress.

"Damn it, I just bought this dress," I muttered as I dipped my napkin in my water and worked at the stain.

"Just be glad the paparazzi hasn't fully started harassing you yet," Beau said as he slapped a copy of one of the smutty gossip magazines on the bar in front of me. I secretly loved gossip magazines and devoured them each week when they were delivered to my mailbox every Thursday.

"What is this trash?" I asked, feigning indifference as I

unsuccessfully tried to dry the now-grapefruit-sized stain on my breast, making me look like I was lactating.

"Oh please – don't even pull that with me, darling. I'm well aware of how much you love your stories," Beau drawled, throwing up his fingers to do air quotes before picking up his clipboard to continue inventory. It was Monday, the one night a week that Lucky's Tiki Bar was closed, and I was Beau's only company as he tallied inventory and prepped for the week ahead. I was enjoying some us time for once. It had been what seemed like ages since we'd spent any time together – not that I was upset with him about it. Beau was in the throes of readying to open his high-end seafood restaurant on the other end of the strip, while also still overseeing the ever-popular Lucky's.

"I suppose I glance at them on occasion," I murmured, peering at the copy of *Celeb Weekly* and noting the date. How had Beau gotten this week's copy so early? I'd have to contact my subscription service.

Then I spied the cover image and almost dropped the rest of my chicken wing down my cleavage.

"You've got to be kidding me," I exclaimed.

"I most certainly wish I was," Beau drawled, poking his head over the bar, amusement dancing across his surfer good looks. More than one woman had been charmed by Beau's handsome face, easy-going manner, and quiet confidence. It usually took either a strong gaydar or a few days spent in his presence before many women picked up on the fact that he didn't bat for their team.

And what a loss it was for the female population, I mused, as I stared at Miss Elva's image beaming back at me from the cover of the glossy magazine. She was posed on my porch – recognizable by my cheerfully painted shutters and my Boston terrier's pointed ears poking over the windowsill. Miss Elva was wearing her now sold-out trucker hat with *I Heart Miss Elva* emblazoned across the front, and a shockingly pink caftan. I was certain her pirate ghost, Rafe, was hovering by her shoulder, though the camera wouldn't have been able to pick him up.

Only a few of us with extra-special abilities could see him anyway.

"Well, she looks good. Pink is a great color for her skin tone," I said, picking up my mojito for a cooling minty sip.

"You've clearly not read the headline," Beau drawled and I choked on a piece of mint as the words registered.

Tequila Key: Psychic Central of the USA? Miss Elva, Althea Rose, and Luna Lavelle Compete for Reigning Queen of the Underworld.

"I'm going to murder her. I swear to god – the fame has gone to her head," I almost shrieked, picking up my phone immediately to text Luna.

Luna's reply was short: *I heard.*

Meet me at Lucky's.

I tried Miss Elva but, as seemed to be the usual for her these days, her phone went straight to voicemail.

"I could put a spell on her, you know. I'm getting better with my magick. Luna's been training me," I said to Beau and he rolled his eyes, shaking his head before he hefted a box into the kitchen, and on my plea, plugged my now-dead phone into a charger before using his broad shoulders to easily push the swinging door open.

"Psychic Central? What is this nonsense," I muttered, paging through the magazine.

I wondered if that made me a hypocrite. I'm Althea Rose and I co-own the Luna Rose Potions & Tarot Shop in sleepy Tequila Key.

And it looked like we'd just been outed to the world.

Available from Amazon

The Isle of Destiny Series

ALSO BY TRICIA O'MALLEY

Stone Song

Sword Song

Spear Song

Sphere Song

A completed series.

Available in audio, e-book & paperback!

"Love this series. I will read this multiple times. Keeps you on the edge of your seat. It has action, excitement and romance all in one series."

- Amazon Review

The Wildsong Series

ALSO BY TRICIA O'MALLEY

Song of the Fae

Melody of Flame

Chorus of Ashes

"The magic of Fae is so believable. I read these books in one sitting and can't wait for the next one. These are books you will reread many times."

- Amazon Review

Available in audio, e-book & paperback!

Available Now

The Siren Island Series

ALSO BY TRICIA O'MALLEY

Good Girl

Up to No Good

A Good Chance

Good Moon Rising

Too Good to Be True

A Good Soul

In Good Time

A completed series.

Available in audio, e-book & paperback!

"Love her books and was excited for a totally new and different one! Once again, she did NOT disappoint! Magical in multiple ways and on multiple levels. Her writing style, while similar to that of Nora Roberts, kicks it up a notch!! I want to visit that island, stay in the B&B and meet the gals who run it! The characters are THAT real!!!" - Amazon Review

The Althea Rose Series

ALSO BY TRICIA O'MALLEY

One Tequila

Tequila for Two

Tequila Will Kill Ya (Novella)

Three Tequilas

Tequila Shots & Valentine Knots (Novella)

Tequila Four

A Fifth of Tequila

A Sixer of Tequila

Seven Deadly Tequilas

Eight Ways to Tequila

Tequila for Christmas (Novella)

"Not my usual genre but couldn't resist the Florida Keys setting. I was hooked from the first page. A fun read with just the right amount of crazy! Will definitely follow this series."- Amazon Review

A completed series.

Available in audio, e-book & paperback!

The Mystic Cove Series

Wild Irish Heart

Wild Irish Eyes

Wild Irish Soul

Wild Irish Rebel

Wild Irish Roots: Margaret & Sean

Wild Irish Witch

Wild Irish Grace

Wild Irish Dreamer

Wild Irish Christmas (Novella)

Wild Irish Sage

Wild Irish Renegade

Wild Irish Moon

"I have read thousands of books and a fair percentage have been romances. Until I read Wild Irish Heart, I never had a book actually make me believe in love."- Amazon Review

A completed series.

Available in audio, e-book & paperback!

Also by Tricia O'Malley

STAND ALONE NOVELS

Ms. Bitch

"Ms. Bitch is sunshine in a book! An uplifting story of fighting your way through heartbreak and making your own version of happily-ever-after."

~Ann Charles, USA Today Bestselling Author

Starting Over Scottish

Grumpy. Meet Sunshine.

She's American. He's Scottish. She's looking for a fresh start. He's returning to rediscover his roots.

One Way Ticket

A funny and captivating beach read where booking a one-way ticket to paradise means starting over, letting go, and taking a chance on love…one more time

10 out of 10 - The BookLife Prize

Contact Me

I hope my books have added a little magick into your life. If you have a moment to add some to my day, you can help by telling your friends and leaving a review. Word-of-mouth is the most powerful way to share my stories. Thank you.

Love books? What about fun giveaways? Nope? Okay, can I entice you with underwater photos and cute dogs? Let's stay friends, receive my emails and contact me by signing up at my website

www.triciaomalley.com

Or find me on Facebook and Instagram.
@triciaomalleyauthor

Made in the USA
Las Vegas, NV
17 December 2024